D0371983

Also by Heinrich Böll

A Soldier's Legacy

▲▲▲▲▲

A Soldier's Legacy

▲▲▲▲▲▲▲

HEINRICH BÖLL

Translated by Leila Vennewitz

ALFRED A. KNOPF NEW YORK 1985

I am deeply grateful to my husband, William, for all
the assistance he has given me in this translation.

LEILA VENNEWITZ

THIS IS A BORZOI BOOK PUBLISHED BY
ALFRED A. KNOPF, INC.

LIBRARY OF CONGRESS CATALOGING
IN PUBLICATION DATA

Böll, Heinrich, [*date*]
A soldier's legacy.
Translation of: Das Vermächtnis.
I. Title.
PT2603.0394V4713   1985   833'.914   84-40724
ISBN 0-394-53603-7

Manufactured in the United States of America
First American Edition

A Soldier's Legacy

▲▲▲▲▲

▲1▲

TODAY, my dear sir, I saw a young man whose name I'm sure is familiar to you; it is Schnecker. He has been living—as far as I know—for a number of years in your neighborhood, and he was a schoolmate of your brother's, who was reported missing during the war. But that's not all. Today I also learned that for five years you have been waiting in vain to discover what actually happened to your brother, after you were informed, by way of that sinister official lie, that he had been "reported missing." Well, Schnecker could have corrected that lie. There are only two people in the world who could have told you with certainty: one is Schnecker, the other is myself. I have kept silent. After reading my report you will understand why I could not come forward and tell you what actually happened.

Forgive me if I must now inform you of something that cannot be glossed over. Your brother is dead.

Actually, when I ran across Schnecker on the terrace of an outdoor café he appeared to be in the best of spirits. He was sitting under one of those colorful umbrellas that are surrounded by planters full of big red geraniums, where customers relax in

the shade as they observe the passing scene from behind their sunglasses. Schnecker was in the company
of a young lady.

The young lady was pretty, her manner light-
hearted and natural. On an impulse, I stepped onto
the terrace, sat down at the next table so I could over-
hear them, and ordered some ice cream.

The shock I felt was intensified by the fact that
Schnecker hadn't changed. He was a bit plumper,
seemed younger rather than older, and showed those
first signs of the incipient bull neck that invariably
begins to manifest itself in certain better-class Germans when they reach thirty-two and are old enough
to take an active part in their father's political party.
After I had thanked the waiter and seated myself so
as to miss nothing, I overheard Schnecker say:

"And Winnie?"

"She's married, didn't you know? She's happy—
deliriously happy, in fact."

Schnecker laughed.

"We'll be, too," he said gently, covering the
girl's hand with his own. The way she turned her
large, soft, slightly stupid eyes up at him made her
look as though she would melt with happiness, leaving behind some kind of sugary mess on the graceful
little terrace chair.

"Cigarette?" asked Schnecker, offering her his
open case. She took one, and they smoked as they

applied themselves to their ice creams. Beyond the terrace a constant stream of perspiring, thinly clad people made their way to or from the summer clearance sales. Their faces revealed a strain similar to what one used to see, only a year ago, on the trains carrying people out into the countryside to scrounge for potatoes—fear, fatigue, greed. Deeply disturbed, I toyed with my ice cream; my cigarette didn't taste good anymore.

"Come to think of it," Schnecker began again, "we have every reason to celebrate today!"

"Yes, today's a red-letter day!" said the girl.

"You're right."

"Of course I'm right! The way you got through it all! So quickly and confidently and the only one to make it with honors. But tell me," she giggled, "are they actually going to put a doctoral cap on your head?"

"No, my dear, but listen." He paused to swallow a spoonful of ice cream. "I suggest we drive out there right away, enjoy ourselves, then change and drive to the Cosmo for a little intimate celebration, before the official stuff gets under way. . . ."

This time she placed her hand on his.

I suddenly felt so nauseated that I had to get up and do something. I left some money on the table, far too much and more than I could possibly afford. But I just didn't care. I staggered outside and let myself drift along with the perspiring, prattling crowd until I turned off onto a quiet, rubble-strewn street that was bathed in the shadow of still-standing façades. I sat down at random on what was left of a wall. The peace of rubble is the peace of graveyards. . . .

It is time, I think, for me to introduce myself. My name is Wenk, and I was a dispatch runner for your brother, First Lieutenant Schelling. I have already told you that he is dead. You could have found that out long ago. You needed only to enter the house of your neighbor and look closely into his eyes, those eyes that will induce such a charming, rhapsodic girl to have him father their two planned children. Oh, that sweet young thing, how she will weep when the priest joins their hands while a Bach fugue resounds from the organ, played not by the regular organist, who is much too pedestrian and inartistic, but by a specially hired musician. Don't fail to attend the wedding. Don't forget to try the cake, the wine and cigars, and make sure your mother offers appropriate congratulations and sends a gift that matches the degree of friendship. This union, from which new Schneckers will spring, must be properly celebrated. I don't know what kind of wedding presents match that degree of friendship in your circles: with us it might be an electric iron,

or a punch bowl that would be used once every three
years or never.

Enough of this chatter! I'm just trying to put off
something I find it hard to write about because it
sounds too improbable in the context of this in-
cipiently bull-necked fledgling Doctor of Laws. But
let me tell you: Schnecker is your brother's murderer.
There it is. There you have it. And I mean it not in
any figurative or allegorical sense, but baldly and
simply, the way I've said it: Schnecker is your
brother's murderer. . . .

You are a young man. About twenty, I would
guess. I have taken the liberty of spending a few afternoons snooping around outside your house and
Schnecker's, but I'm sure you won't remember that
nondescript individual standing under an elderberry
tree, wearing sunglasses and smoking a cigarette, a
sort of amateur detective of fate who, in return for a
pension of thirty marks graciously doled out to him
every month at the post office, feels obliged to render
the Fatherland a small service.

Well, you're twenty, I would guess. I saw you
hurrying off with your book-filled briefcase at regular
hours and fancied I could read something in your expression that I can only interpret as: dread of your
finals. Don't worry, you'll get through all right. Don't
take it too seriously. We were still priding ourselves

on getting a B in geography and math when we were forced to look at men who had just been neatly shot in the stomach by a machine-gun salvo. Believe me, they all looked alike, those who had a B in Latin and those who had never heard of Latin. They looked ugly; there was nothing, absolutely nothing uplifting about them. They were all alike—Poles, Germans, and Frenchmen, heroes and cowards. That's all I can tell you. They belonged to the earth, and the earth no longer belonged to them. That's all. . . .

But before I tell you how Schnecker killed your brother, I must introduce myself in greater detail. I'm not exactly a confidence-inspiring person. Most of my time is spent lying on the bed smoking cigarettes. The venetian blinds are kept closed, letting in just enough light for me to tell which side of the cigarette paper is gummed. Next to the bed is my chair, on it a great heap of loose yellow tobacco. I occupy myself by rolling a new cigarette when the butt between my lips has become damp and no longer draws. The tobacco makes my throat burn, I flick the butts out the window, and whenever I lean out I can see great quantities of them floating in the roof gutter—burst, yellowish objects like bloated maggots; from some of them the tobacco has seeped out and is floating in the greenish soupy liquid filling the gutter that slopes away from the drain. Sometimes, when

this scum has grown too thick, I borrow the broom
belonging to my landlord's cleaning woman and
sweep all the sludge toward the drain, where with a
low gurgling sound it disappears. . . .

I am very seldom persuaded to undertake any
kind of activity. My one great concern is how to get
hold of tobacco, which I pay for by selling my books.
Even this activity is strenuous enough. Fortunately I
am fairly well informed as to the value of the books,
although I must say I lack the patience to insist on
getting their true value. So I reluctantly drag myself
off to those dingy little secondhand bookstores that
smell of the decay which only piles of books produce:
dry, musty, moldy. Skinny yellow hands, whose movements remind me of the silent, repulsive haste of
raccoons, assess my spiritual property according to
its material value. I rarely haggle, only when the offer
seems unreasonably low; otherwise I merely nod and
remain adamant when the usurer thrusts his pitiful
face toward me as he counts out the money, hoping to
persuade me at the last moment to accept less. I have
resigned myself to the fact that I can no more cope
with these people than I could with the war.

▲2▲

I FIRST MET Schnecker in the summer of 1943. I
had been ordered to leave an interpreter unit sta-
tioned in Paris and report to a coastal division where
I was once again to partake of the joys of "real" infantry service. Leaving the last railway station behind me, I had reached a sleepy little place that
seemed to consist of long, low walls surrounding lush
grass. There, in the northwestern corner of Normandy,
parallel to the coast, runs a strip of land that breathes
the brooding isolation of heath and marsh: here and
there a few tiny hamlets, some abandoned, ruined
farms, shallow streams meandering sluggishly toward
the swampy arms of the Somme or petering out underground.

From the station I had laboriously asked my way
to battalion headquarters. There, predictably, I had
been kept waiting a considerable time before being
directed to one of the companies. The clerk, a corporal, suggested I wait for the mail orderly of my
future unit and go along with him. But since that
would have meant a four-hour wait outside this deso-
late château, I asked the corporal how to get there,
saluted, and left.

As I was shouldering my pack in the dark corridor, an officer passed by, a tall slim fellow who, in spite of his youth, was wearing the insignia of a captain. I performed the infamous "salute by standing at attention": he looked at me as if I were made of glass and, without so much as a nod, walked on. It was Schnecker.

Only half a second had passed, but in that half second I felt all the humiliation forced upon us by the uniform. Every second I wore that uniform I hated it, but now I was so choked by disgust I actually felt a bitter taste on my tongue. I hurried after the officer, who was walking toward the orderly room, and planted myself in front of him, thus preventing him from reaching the door handle. I stood at attention again and said: "I request the captain to acknowledge my salute." My loathing filled me with voluptuous pleasure. He looked at me as if I had gone out of my mind.

"What was that?" he asked huskily.

I repeated my words in an even tone, saluted again, looked at him, saluted again.

The battle was fought only between our eyes. He was fuming, ready to tear me to pieces, but from the ends of my coolly vibrating hair right down to my toes I was filled with a crystalline hatred. He suddenly raised his hand to his cap; I stood aside, opened the door for him, and walked away.

I passed quickly through the lethargic, sleeping

village, took, as directed, the third turning on the left
toward the coast, and soon found myself in a completely uninhabited area. Noonday heat quivered over
the meadows, the road was dusty and stony, there
were occasional little groups of trees, lots of bushes,
no fields that I could see. I took advantage of the little
shade there was and walked on for half an hour; then
I suddenly stopped, looked up, and realized that all
that time I had been staring unseeingly ahead of me.
I was tired and suddenly felt quite exhausted. The
roadside was covered with lush grass, but just as I
was about to sit down I noticed, scarcely a hundred
yards away, a larger group of trees that seemed to
indicate a building. In the sultry heat the cows had
sought the shade of the bushes. I walked along the
flagstone path and stopped outside the building: it
was very dilapidated, surrounded by tangled growth,
the windows were blind, and above the door was a
weathered sign, almost illegible, on which I could
just make out the letters AURAN of the word RESTAU-
RANT.

The door was open: I walked into a stale-smelling
passageway and opened a brown door on the right.
The room was empty. I put down my pack, threw
cap and belt onto a chair, pulled out my big hand-
kerchief, and began to wipe the sweat off my face as
I looked around.

In taverns like this, one automatically expects a

sour old witch of a woman, moustached, dirty, who can offer only some lukewarm stuff. I was very surprised when a young girl, who was not only pretty but clean, came in and greeted me briefly but without hostility with the usual "Good morning, sir."

I returned her greeting and looked at her much too long. She was very lovely. Her brown eyes were large, slightly veiled, and seemed always to look away. Her reddish-brown hair fell loosely over her shoulders and was tied above her forehead with a blue ribbon. Her hands gave off a smell of milk and udders, her fingers were still spread, slightly curled. . . .

"What would you like?" she asked.

I wanted to say "You!" but with a gesture stopped myself and said quietly: "Something to drink, something cold perhaps."

She closed her eyes and seemed to be letting my unspoken word sink into her; then she raised her lids again and said mockingly: "Wine or lemonade?"

"Water," I said.

"I wouldn't recommend it, sir," she said. "Our water is as foul as the Somme."

"All right," I said, "wine, then: white if you have some."

She nodded, turned, and disappeared.

The place was furnished like most country taverns in France. It used to be customary to dismiss them as being fusty, tasteless, uninviting. True, they did contain a lot of kitsch, both old and modern, but for me every one of those taverns held something of the elusive appeal of Cézanne's card players.

The girl's pale face loomed up behind the glass panel, almost like the face of a drowning person rising to the surface once more before sinking for the last time. Quickly I jumped up and opened the door for her. In her right hand she was balancing a bottle of wine and a glass, in her left a soda-water siphon. To my astonishment the siphon, which I took from her, was cool. I commented on it, and while she set down glass and bottle she explained that they always kept the siphons in the well. As she spoke she avoided looking at me and murmured: "If you need anything, just call." She was about to leave.

I said very softly: "Tell me one thing: are you always here? Are you the owner's daughter?"

Now for the first time she turned and looked at me. I had the impression she was smiling.

"Yes," she said, "I'm always here."

"Well, then I'd like to pay. I'll take the rest of the bottle along, if I may—who knows whether there's anything available out there?" I pointed toward the coast.

"There are some taverns there, too," she said indifferently, shrugging her shoulders, "but if you like . . ."

She went to the counter, and it seemed to me she did so merely in order to avoid touching my hand, for in taverns like that the money isn't paid formally at a cash register but simply passes from hand to hand. She gave me my change and said coolly: "Good-bye, sir." I was alone. It was good to know that she had said: I'm always here. I sat down, stretched out my legs, ate, drank, and smoked. After finishing half the bottle I stood up, adjusted my pack, called in the direction of the door leading to the rear, "Good-bye!" and left.

The road was uneven and tiring, there wasn't a soul in sight, just meadows with streams trickling away into them, shrubs, clumps of willows, until finally in the distance I made out a straight row of trees that seemed to indicate the coast road. I took another breather, smoked a cigarette under that dull gray sky, and then walked toward the pale, bluish silhouette of the row of trees. . . .

▲3▲

I PROMISE not to become too garrulous. Nothing of what I am telling you is irrelevant if you happen to be interested in your brother's fate, in the part played by Schnecker and, to some extent, in my per-

son. I can no longer keep silent. Fear and dread have
taken hold of me since I have had to cast a brief but
enlightening glance behind the rosy façade of the
German "restoration" and "restitution," a glance into
Schnecker's face. The face of an average person.

I forgot to tell you that I don't care for the sun.
There are times when I believe I hate it. If I were to
worship any of the idols of ancient or primitive peo-
ples, I would choose to join those somber-minded
tribes who offer tribute to the sun as a devil rather
than those who venerate it as a god. I don't hate the
light—I love light shining in the darkness, but that
harsh summer sun—sheer light—that is something
cruel.

The highway I soon reached was flanked only on
the right by a row of trees whose shadow fell on open
country, a meadow covered by lush, shoulder-high
grass. It was only later that I discovered that all the
meadows on both sides of the road were mined; left
and right, grass and flowers grew with a luxuriance I
had never seen before. A few fir saplings were dotted
about. For three years no hand had been able to mow
or care for those meadows, and no cattle had been
able to browse in them.

Somewhere up ahead I had caught sight of a
building at what seemed to be an intersection in the
shady forest, but that bright sunshine not only daz-
zled me, it induced in me an almost demoralizing

physical pain. The distance seemed endless, although
it couldn't have been more than three hundred meters.
After five minutes I reached the building. Another
tavern. Scattered about the fir forest were attractive
little modern houses, and along the road some other
houses. At the intersection stood a little signpost that
said "BLANCHÈRES." The tavern bore a newly painted
sign saying "BUVETTE À L'ORIENT." I stepped inside
and right away, without looking around, put down my
pack and began to wipe the sweat off my face again.

As I gradually came to from my exhaustion, I
found myself looking into a terrible face, which was
smiling at me. I am sure you don't know about those
creatures that live on the other, the seldom described
side of war. Our patriotic literature has no room for
reality.

The broad face was heavily coated with powder,
the large, pale-blue eyes were bleary, below the eyes
were terrible bags. It was the Blanchères tavern's
landlady. She, too, played a major role in your
brother's life: she washed his laundry, which was so
important to him, and she washed it thoroughly and
was cheap.

"Hullo, soldier," she said to me in a surprisingly
deep voice. "Have a seat," she added.

"Good afternoon, Madame," I said.

"Oh," she cried, "I'm not Madame, I'm Mademoiselle!"

"Good afternoon, Mademoiselle," I said.

"What'll you have?"

I had sat down on one of the chairs near the door.

"Beer, please, if you have any."

So far I had seen only her head and automatically assumed her to be fat. It was a shock, when she now approached me, armed with a bottle of beer and a glass, to see that she was as skinny as an old hen, frighteningly ugly.

"Santé!" she said, without moving away. "You're new here?"

"Yes," I said, "I'm on my way to company headquarters."

"Oh, with that heavy pack?"

"Yes."

"Then wait a bit." She looked up at an old-fashioned clock hanging over the bar. "Just wait, the orderly from over in Larnton will be here any minute." She pointed down the road that led off to the left, whereas according to my instructions I should have walked straight on for another kilometer.

"He comes at four and has a bicycle. He'll take your pack. He's a nice fellow. You're joining the infantry, aren't you?"

"Yes," I said. I was surprised at how well informed she was. I looked at the clock: it was a few minutes to four.

Her eyes were almost bursting with curiosity. The main occupation of these creatures is to collect tidbits of news. They are just as garrulous and observant as their sisters of the other kind: the devout church-goers. She continued the conversation, as promptly as a skilled journalist embarking on an interview.

"Your sergeant is a good man," she said; "the C.O. is a swine. You'll see. And that one down there" —she pointed presumably to a base—"is an angel. He is," she added firmly, as if I had been about to contradict her.

"Oh?" I merely said, drily.

"Where've you come from?" she went on with hardly a break, the curiosity in her eyes now coupled with a kind of impertinence.

"From Paris."

"Ah," she cried again in her rough voice. "Where love reigns supreme!" I said nothing.

"Almost all of them nice fellows, your company," she prattled on. "In fact, the infantry's fine any place. Poor and fine, that's what I always say. . . ."

All this time my eyes had been fixed on the road that looked to me like a haven of peace and shade. It was bordered by dense pine forests that were flecked with pale, sandy patches heralding the prox-imity of the dunes. On either side of the road, at ir-regular intervals, stood charming little houses, but it was a while before I noticed that this whole area, too, was marked off by mine fences and mine warnings. So that explained this graveyard silence.

"How about giving me one?" she suddenly asked, looking at my package of cigarettes.

"Oh, excuse me!" I said.

"You're certainly generous with your tobacco—let's see what you're like in a couple of weeks!" I had said nothing although she had taken two cigarettes. "Tobacco is as scarce as hen's teeth hereabouts." To my relief I at last saw a cyclist in uniform rapidly approaching out of the shadowy depths of the avenue. He was carrying his rifle, in the regulation manner, with its strap across his chest.

"Ah," she cried, "there he is! Willi!"

She stepped outside and waved to the approaching soldier, whose face I could now plainly see. He was a pale, middle-aged man; his fair moustache, narrow and sparse, looked as if it was stuck onto his upper lip. He was wearing his cap, too, like a new recruit, and there was something eager about his expression.

He dismounted, propped his bicycle outside the door, and came in.

"Hullo there," he said.

"Hullo," I answered.

Willi looked enviously at the girl's cigarette, then

at me, climbed onto a bar stool, and asked: "Did you manage to get some more cigarettes on the black market?"

"No," she said, "I'm supposed to get some to-morrow, cheap, seven francs each."

"What about that one?"

She pointed the lighted cigarette at me. I had already fished out my package and was offering it to Willi. He gave me a surprised look, laughed shortly, and said: "Thanks a lot—you must've come straight from home, but then they don't have that much there either. . . ."

"No," I said, "but are you that short here?"

"I'll say we are," he said, "you'll find out. We wait every day with our tongues hanging out for our three rationed cigarettes, but they're gone in an hour, then the butts, and then another twenty-three hours' craving."

"Want a drink?" asked the girl.

"Yes, please, Cadette, a beer."

"Here's to you," he then said. "To your ciga-rettes, mate. . . ."

I paid when he did, seeing that he had quickly downed his beer and wanted to be off; I stepped up to the counter beside him as he put on his cap again. "D'you think you could take my stuff along?" I asked.

Assuming a rather ponderous expression, he

looked first at my pack and bag and then said: "Mind you, it's a pretty wobbly old bike, an old rattletrap, but O.K."—he made a great show of squaring his shoulders—"I wouldn't let a fellow soldier kill himself for nothing. So you're joining our outfit?"

"Yes," I said, "third company."

"Right, third, that's us. O.K., let's get your stuff loaded."

Feeling very envious, I watched him sail off. Fortunately the road was shady. On the left was dense forest, starting at Cadette's house and bordering the road, and to the right side of the smooth asphalt road stood a few houses, apparently still occupied. Next to one of them some soldiers' washing was hanging on a line: shirts, underpants, and the kind of socks—gray with horizontal white stripes—that are scattered over half the world. I hurried along, for, in addition to some nervousness about my new duties, I also felt a certain curiosity. There was always something exciting about a transfer. I still hadn't caught sight of the sea, but on the map shown me by the sergeant at battalion headquarters the dot indicating the company's orderly room had been very close to that stirring dot-and-dash line marked "Main Battle Line—High Tide Line." I was impatient to see the sea again after three years.

Five minutes later the forest came to an end. On both sides of the road, those lush meadows again, and

at last, beyond a gentle rise, I saw the house beside
a sandy path. It looked quite charming, like a rich
man's comfortable weekend cottage. To the right of
the road was another tavern, a kind of summer café
built of wood with a covered veranda; in the background, more buildings; then for the first time since
noon I saw sergeants' stars again among corporals'
braid—a bunch of soldiers standing around a field
kitchen, and all romantic notions of a lovely summer on the Atlantic coast vanished. I saluted a few
sergeants who were standing by a shed watching the
food distribution, and finally I reached the orderly
room.

After walking up a few steps, the first thing I saw
was my pack lying on the floor. There was a per-
vasive, musty smell of heat and dry timbers. I heard
voices, among them Willi's calling out "Here!" some-
place where mail was evidently being distributed. I
entered the room that had a sign saying: "Field Post
Office No. ————." Well, that was the number I was to
see so often on the postcards I later accepted here for
your brother and took to Larnton. For you, too, that
number must be unforgettable.

After completing the ritual of saluting at the door,
I immediately heard a voice speaking in a Saxonian
accent. I looked in that direction and saw a first lieutenant whose curly coal-black hair was cut in a rather
fancy style, and my first impression was that the little

red ribbon of his Iron Cross set off his glossy hair to
a T. He looked about forty, and he, too, had a moustache, a black one, and at the sight of that black
moustache it crossed my mind how magnificently that
black in turn set off the silver of his Assault Medal.

"Aha," said this person on catching sight of me,
not as if he were bawling me out but rather in a re-
proachful, schoolmasterly tone, and indeed half an
hour later I learned that he was a schoolteacher. At
the same time I became aware of the not unfriendly
face of a first sergeant, still young, and the impassive
countenance of a clerk who looked pleasant enough.

So, "Aha," said this person, "here we have the
lord and master who feels too weak to carry his pack
for a distance of one kilometer—right?"

With his last words he opened his eyes wide, giving them a theatrical glint, and looked at me chal-
lengingly.

"Sir!" I said, standing to attention. "I could see
no point in letting my comrade ride an empty bicycle
while I carried the pack that I had already lugged
all the way from Crutelles."

"All the way from Crutelles!" he repeated sarcastically. The topkick burst out laughing.

"Don't laugh, Fischer," the first lieutenant
snapped at him. "These goddam intellectual swine
who've been on special assignment for years are a
cheeky bunch." Then he turned to me. "So you, a Pfc,

take the liberty of thinking, using your head, if I have understood you properly—hm?"

I had become so accustomed to quasi-civilian manners that I almost nodded and said: "That's right." I suppressed it and uttered the regulation "Yessir."

"I see. And weren't you taught the opposite, that you're not supposed to use your head—hm?"

"No," I replied, "in my last unit I was sometimes required to use my head."

"Well!" he said, surprised, and for a moment he looked like a boxer on the receiving end of a well-placed blow. But suddenly he bellowed: "There'll be none of that here, d'you hear me? No more thinking, understand? No more using your head, get it?"

"Yessir," I said.

"And what's more, remember that a soldier never allows himself to be separated from his pack." He turned his cheap, fiery gaze away from me, toward the topkick, and asked brusquely: "Where'll we put him?" The topkick pulled a list out of a drawer, and the first lieutenant turned his Storm Trooper eyes back to me (I later found out that he really had been a platoon leader with the Storm Troopers in his home town). "What training have you had?" he asked me. "I mean military, of course."

"Rifleman," I said, "sir, and telephone operator."

"Balls," he said furiously, "we have enough telephone operators, never enough riflemen."

"It's Larnton's turn for replacements," said the topkick.

"Good. We'll send him to Mister Schelling. Anything else? Tomorrow's schedule is clear, ammunition to be taken to the base for live firing. O.K.?"

"Yessir," said the topkick.

I flung open the door, stood at attention, and stepped aside for the schoolteacher. He did not deign to look my way again.

"For Chrissake!" cried the topkick when the sound of footsteps outside had died away. "I could've hugged you when I heard you were from the Rhineland!"

He shook my hand, I looked into his face and felt glad. He pointed to the clerk, who was watching us with a smile.

"Schmidt," he said, "at least Schmidt's from Berlin. We do have a few fellows from Berlin, but otherwise they're a bunch of yokels."

I handed him the envelope containing my papers that I had closed and sealed myself. The clerk opened it, read and sorted the papers, the topkick asked me how things were at home, when I had last seen Cologne, his home town, and when I'd been on leave.

Soon after that he left for supper, and I was alone with the pleasant clerk. I asked him about the general atmosphere, the daily routine, exchanged a few mutual, sceptical observations about the war and the company commander, and fifteen minutes later I found myself walking back along the same road. Again I stopped by Cadette's, again I had a beer and gave her a cigarette.

Then I walked down that avenue that had so fascinated me. I still hadn't caught sight of the sea—from the orderly room it had been hidden by the forest; besides, I had been looking at the first lieutenant's pale-gray uniform.

But it was bound to come soon now. The road ran like a narrow ribbon between the minefields, and I felt as if I were running straight into a trap. On both sides stood attractive little houses, their gardens run wild, then the road opened up, and on the left there appeared a fair-sized, completely pillaged building that looked like a school. At last I saw the pale strip of beach. . . . There was hardly any water to be seen, the coast being so flat at that point that at low tide the sea receded for a kilometer or more. In the distance —indescribably far away, it seemed—I saw a pale, broad tongue, the narrow wave of foam that the sea pushes ahead or drags behind itself, and beyond that an equally narrow strip of gray: the water. And otherwise only sand, sand, and the pale sky that was also burned gray. I felt an uprush of disappointment at having landed in a dry infinity, for when I pulled back my gaze from the distance into which it had plunged, all I saw close by, too, was sand, dunes

sparsely covered with grass, and among them the
ruins of houses that had obviously been dynamited—
and more sand. . . .

And nowhere was there the bunker I had expected
to find. Fortunately a soldier with a rifle was standing on a dune next to a spiked barrier across the road;
a concrete path led up to him. I followed it. The steel
helmet and the muzzle of the rifle grew bigger and
more distinct, and on reaching the top I discovered a
strange little colony. It looked almost like a fishing
village where the nets are hung up to dry in the evening. These were camouflage nets covering guns and
barracks, and the wooden huts were part of the famous
Atlantic Wall in the summer of 1943 at a strategi-
cally vulnerable point. I walked toward the sentry,
and when I asked him where I could find Lieutenant
Schelling he pointed with a bored expression at a hut
slightly higher up, but before I had reached it he
called after me: "By the way, it's *First* Lieutenant,
bud, don't get it wrong!"

"What?" I asked.

"He's a first lieutenant—not that he cares, but
that's what he is. You might as well know."

I was amazed to find a first lieutenant heading a
platoon. In 1943, officers were pretty thin on the
ground, and it seemed extraordinary to me that this
tiny base, which could, if necessary, have been in the

charge of a sergeant, should be under the command of a first lieutenant.

The first person I saw as I entered the hut was Willi. He was alone, reading a letter.

"Ah," he exclaimed, "they've sent you to us!"

"Yes."

Willi laid the letter aside, pushing it under a telephone: he had opened the window, and there was a breeze from the sea.

"Let's see," said Willi, "if the First Lieutenant is available." He knocked on the door, someone called out—reluctantly, it seemed to me—"Come in!", Willi opened the door and into the darkened room announced my arrival. A croaky voice said: "Very well—show him in." I stepped inside and closed the door behind me.

The window was covered by a blanket, and I could vaguely make out a bed with a long, gray figure lying on it, a cupboard, a table, and a few unidentifiable pictures on the walls.

I felt enormously heartened by the way this man immediately stood up as I entered. That may seem trivial to you, but, believe me, when one's been a soldier in this army for many years, always having to deal with so-called superiors, one develops an infallible instinct for the forms of human relationships. If you knew how many of your friends—I need only think of my own, or take any pleasant young man who you're sure would never hurt a fly—if you knew how he used to behave toward so-called inferiors, I believe you would blush with shame on his behalf. . . .

Your brother was the first officer I ran across in five years of whom I can claim that he moved with complete confidence on the narrow borderline of simultaneous authority and humility, as befits a superior. No doubt you're familiar with the other kind, those pipsqueak lieutenants: totally ignorant, brainless, and not even competent in their military, let alone soldierly, craft, sustained solely by the authority of their two shoulder straps and, last but not least, of their elegant boots. And you may grasp the extent of the uniform's demonic power from the fact that this huge army relied exclusively on this idiotic perversion of values, for even before 1943 the original illusory conception had proven as void and insubstantial as a wizened toy balloon lying trampled on a fairground.

Try to imagine any one of your brother's many contemporaries or classmates—leaving aside Schnecker—any one of them, I say, a nice kind man whose behavior is invariably decent and blameless, and I tell you: in the barracks he's a swine! And that army carted its barracks all across Europe. . . .

That's how X and Y were: X who today stifles his

bitterness over his temporarily obsolete career with American cigarettes and vague political aspirations, meanwhile getting together regularly with his former comrades to reminisce about how they used to "show them a thing or two"; and Y who is grimly preparing himself to become a district attorney or a high-school teacher—either of which occupations offers enough scope for bullying creatures even more defenseless than soldiers: children and the poor.

▲4▲

Your brother, as I said, got up from his bed for me. I need hardly describe him to you: tall and slim, with a slight stoop at that time, his blue eyes full of sadness, his uniform bare of any decorations. He was about my age, twenty-five or -six, and, although it may seem ridiculous to you, a first lieutenant's star on that figure seemed to me fraught with ominous significance. A first lieutenant on that tiny base in the dunes, with a garrison of twenty-five men, the commander of a bastion which at that stage of the war could well have been entrusted to a sergeant: there must be some story behind that.

He repeated my name in his rather husky voice.

"You will remain here," he said after looking me briefly in the eyes. "I need an orderly, my present one is going on leave tomorrow. Do you understand?"

"Yessir," I said.

"Good. Please have yourself briefed. You will share telephone duty with the stretcher-bearer. In addition, you will be required to make two bicycle trips a day to company headquarters. And then"—he was silent for a moment and looked at me again— "you will have noticed on the way here that we are in a mousetrap, and no one is allowed to leave it other than on duty without my knowledge. There's no such thing as time off. Do you understand?"

"Yessir," I said.

"Good. Please have the orderly explain all practical matters to you."

His eyes met mine again. I took this for a silent dismissal, saluted, and left.

On this front of the Atlantic coast, my dear sir, a very special kind of warfare was being carried on, the war against boredom. Try to imagine a front extending from Norway to the Bay of Biscay and facing no opponent other than the sea. And this front was equipped like any other where each day saw wounded and dead, men screaming and dying, men horrifyingly mute. But here everything was completely fro-

zen. Night after night, thousands of soldiers stood on
guard waiting for an enemy who never came and
whose coming some of them positively craved. Year
after year, night after night, thousands stood there
facing the sea, that monster which is eternally the
same, eternally the same, comes and goes, comes and
goes, is always smiling, always smiling with a serenity
fit to induce a man to plunge headlong into it. An
eternal smile; the sea, even when storm-tossed, always had something like laughter about it, wild
laughter devoid of mockery, but still laughter. The
sea was laughing at us, that was it. There stood the
guns, mortars, machine guns; rifles by the hundred
thousand lay there on parapets or were lugged back
and forth by plodding sentries. Nothing. Year after
year the same. Every evening a password to be mem-
orized plus the various flare signals, hand grenades
placed in readiness—hand grenades against the sea!
During the day, instruction in the use of guns, mortars, machine guns and other weapons, and drill on
the road behind the dunes, year after year. Year after
year. During the day, almost eight hours' duty, and
at night at least four hours' sentry duty. The never
ending battle against the sand that relentlessly pene-
trated the farthest, most inaccessible crack of every
weapon and never failed to be discovered by some
bored corporal's eye. And somewhere beyond the
horizon, far, far, incredibly far away, there was an

enemy in whom it was impossible to believe—far, far away, an enemy from whom the sea seemed to have learned its laughter. All that lay like a pall of apathy over even the most idyllic little bays, driving us to drink.

Some of the men had been at it since 1940. But even those who had known it only for a few months were beginning to show signs of despair. Despair is the hope of the flesh, my dear sir. There is a kind of despair that, even if it exists only in the mind, is a wild, sensual pleasure. Despair has something of the substance of a movie. One drinks it, it is sweet, sweet, so sweet that one wants to drink up a whole sea of it, but the more one drinks the thirstier one becomes, the more convinced that this thirst is unquenchable, that perhaps here on earth one is already in Hell, for Hell might somehow be that perpetual thirst. Despair is terrible, despair is the hope of the flesh, and one might feel tempted to pray: Lead us not into despair.

Even a person like your brother, who was always assured of the consolations of his faith, whose strength was such that he could have spent his whole life walking along a knife edge, ultimately to leap from its utmost point into eternal bliss—even a person like your brother was feeling the gnawings of this despair when I arrived. During the first few days I was there, I observed in the melancholy expression of his eyes a vague something that almost reminded me of a per-

son about to go berserk. Often, while he was on the
phone talking to that schoolmaster, there was a quiver
in his voice as if he were at breaking point, about to
cry out: Nitwit, nitwit, nitwit! Incorrigible nitwit!

Well, I was as weak as he was strong. And I was
no longer accustomed to any kind of hardship. I had
brought off the seemingly impossible: in the uniform
of an ordinary soldier I had managed to lead a life to
my own liking. My firsthand experience of the war
dated from 1940, when I had felt the urge for closer
acquaintance after spending two years in barracks
undergoing training as an infantryman. After those
six weeks of campaign, I had had enough of war. Dust
and dirt and heat, permanently painful, burning feet,
blood, and a lot of hysteria, and, to crown it all, the
worst part: helping those repulsive banners of the
Nazis to invade the garden that was France. Not for
me. Just four days before the Armistice I was
wounded in southern France, on the border of Bur-
gundy. I recovered, hung around for months in a
military hospital, and, by bluffing a bit with my
school French, contrived to have myself transferred
to Paris. In those days a wounded soldier was still a
hero. Having succeeded in getting to Paris, I made
the most of my illness in order, as we used to say, to
maintain the position.

To some extent I had been looking forward to this
new tour of duty on the coast, the way one always

starts out looking forward to something new. But after
a few days I was on the brink of despair.

The futility was appalling. There stood the men
every morning with their machine guns or mortars,
drilling, drilling, in the sand dunes, practicing the
movements they had ceased to master because they
had been practicing them for too long. They were personally acquainted with almost every grain of sand.
And every morning the same, every night the same,
and always only the one enemy, the sea; all around
them, minefields, empty buildings. And not even
enough to eat. Not even enough to eat to keep up their
strength. Food is an essential part of war. Every sensible officer knows that. The waging of war knows no
romanticism; there is no place anywhere for so-called
ideas or emotions. A soldier who is permanently hungry is capable of the worst, and he is fully justified
in obtaining whatever food he can. The rations were
simply ridiculous, my dear sir. I know you aren't
aware of that. How often have I carried postcards
from the men that said: "Alive and well, thanks for
the parcel. Heinrich."

Picture, if you can, a man who spends eight hours
a day on duty plus four hours a night on sentry duty,
living on a pound of bread, two spoonfuls of jam, an
ounce of margarine and, at midday, a quart of soup
made from water and cauliflower in which, for a hundred and fifty men, a quarter of a skeleton of a

scrawny cow has been boiled after being stripped by the mess cook of its last vestiges of meat and fat. Maybe you think that's a lot. It's nothing when a man is fighting boredom.

Well, we found ways to help ourselves. We kept back ammunition and exchanged it for bread with overfed marines and gunners who could find the time to go rabbit-hunting. In that area the navy had its own farms, and at night, whenever we were off duty, we would sneak out onto the potato fields, eluding the sentries who were guarding the crops with cocked rifles, and in the darkness we would grub around in the soil, like wild boar, to fill up our sacks. And don't believe we had any romantic notions about exposing ourselves to the risk of being shot at, for the sentries did fire whenever they caught sight of us.

So you can add hunger to boredom, and just remember that your brother fought for three years on this front.

On the morning of the third day, as I awoke, the stale air fell like lead into my lungs. The room was full of smoke; the stretcher-bearer had, as always, fallen asleep at the phone, his stupid head lying in a flattened tin can that we used for an ashtray. Naturally, as the latest arrival, I occupied the less desirable of the two bunks, the upper one, and, not yet used to the low ceiling, I would absentmindedly sit up every morning and bump my head painfully against the ceiling. I looked at my watch: it was six-thirty. So once again he was an hour late for his wake-up duty.

The soldiers were stubborn, fighting tooth and nail for every minute of sleep. And they had every right, for they never had a single night of unbroken sleep, and what can be more ghastly than to be wrenched night after night out of profound sleep?

The night sentries were allowed to go off duty at six a.m., unless it happened to be high tide, which always meant an intensified state of alert. If they wanted, they could grab some extra sleep until seven-thirty before getting ready to go on duty again. In order not to leave the coast totally unguarded during the next two hours, a single so-called day sentry was posted for the entire base. This sentry had to stand on higher ground, was equipped with an alarm signal, and had to leave his post at eight a.m. to take part in the day's regular duties. It was the orderly's job to wake that sentry. And you can take my word for it that not a single one of the night sentries, even if he happened to be lying in the bunk next to the day sentry, would have lifted a finger to wake him. It was the orderly's job, and if the orderly failed to do so, too bad, then the base was left unguarded, and the Tommies or the Yanks could come if they ever had a mind to do so.

So the base was left unguarded. During the first three days I took all this fairly seriously. I really did think the British were coming, and when I woke up in the morning around that hour—which was unquestionably the most favorable for a potential attack—I had a vision of landing barges gliding silently up onto the beach, their troops leaping from the bow—and Hurrah!

So I jumped up, poked the stretcher-bearer in the ribs, and said: "Get up, you have to wake the sentry!"

That stretcher-bearer was one of the stupidest fellows I have ever met. He was middle-aged, forty-two years old, with crinkly hair and a thick, impenetrable skull and tiny, drink-sodden eyes. He was almost always asleep, and not only could he hardly write German—in his mouth even the spoken language became a very limited means of communication.

"Ah," he said, rubbing his eyes, "I sleeping, I goddamn sleeping, first time happen."

"O.K.," I said, "first time happen, but get going now, it's time." He fumbled for a slip of paper lying under the telephone, held it up close to his eyes, and silently committed the name to memory. Then he put on his cap to leave, but I knew that he often woke up the wrong man—more than once we had barely saved him from being beaten up by his victim—so I took the slip and repeated aloud: "Pellerig, Bunker 4, first bunk left of the door, lower."

"What?" He heaved himself around. "I thinking Brunswick."

"No," I said. "Brunswick has to go to the orderly room, he's going on leave."

"O.K." He left.

I lit a cigarette, ran my fingers through my hair, and stepped out the door. It was wonderful outside. A cool, gentle wind came from the sea, whose foamy, lapping tongue had halted quite close to our hut, at the foot of a sand dune. It was high tide, the water was blue-gray, and there was a genuine smell of the sea. I stared at that endless surface, that grandiose plain of water, watched the seagulls, and shielded my eyes with my hand so as to savor the solitude. Perhaps I could make out a coast guard vessel; it was always a pleasure to see the ocean enlivened by some rare vessel. The weather was overcast, the sun, behind me, lay wrapped up in a thick gray cloud. To the north, the view was hidden by the same pine forest that stretched from Cadette's tavern all the way to the coast. I had been told that one could see the mouth of the Somme by walking to the edge of the forest. I decided to give it a try that afternoon during a free half hour. So somewhere to the northwest was England . . . one could sail across the sea, and suddenly an island would appear—England. . . .

I kept my eye on Kandick, the stretcher-bearer, and made sure he went into the correct bunker. Everything was silent, soft vaporous banks of morning fog lay above the dunes and huts. It was the only truly peaceful hour of the day here.

Suddenly a voice behind me said: "Good morning." I turned, stood at attention, and saluted.

Your brother made a wry face. "Let's not have any of that, please." I had been embarrassed too, but somehow or other I had to respond to his greeting, and I had already spent too long in the prison of my uniform to allow myself the liberty of a simple "Good morning," as one summer visitor to another. He noticed my embarrassment. "I know, that's what you were taught. But it's not appropriate here, and there's no need, is there? If you like, you can say 'Good morning' to me. I'd be sorry if I'd offended you, but I think we understand each other. . . ."

I looked aside. "The point is," he went on, "I know that you find it repugnant—so do I."

He took out a cigarette and lit it from mine, then sat down on a little bench outside the entrance to our bunker. Those first minutes in the morning, when one stepped outside, saw the sea, felt the wind and the glorious air, when everything was still silent—those first minutes were beautiful. But the specter of daily duty was too real, too deeply ingrained in our memory, for us to be able to linger over our pleasure. Monotony is the most effective weapon of modern warfare.

"You know," he began again, "I'm told there are parents who greet their sleepy children in the morning with a snappy 'Heil Hitler.' There really are such people, just imagine." His expression was somber. "Can you imagine anything more sickening?"

As I already told you, my despair had become greater after three days than that of your brother after three years. I am a weak person, I had no prop, no religion, only a very vague, ephemeral dream of a certain beauty and order. And yet on that particular morning we two were, I believe, on the same level with our despair. For three years he had swum alone against that sluggish tide of monotony and horror, I had leaped into that mire only three days before, and, filled with the same fear, we were both struggling against being swallowed up by it. We were each like a swimmer who, believing himself alone and lost in a vast body of water, suddenly looks around and finds someone at his side.

I looked at him. That remark about the Hitler salute was so daring that it put him completely at my mercy, at a time when one could be sentenced to death for even dreaming about *lèse majesté*.

I said: "Sir, I believe we share the same opinion."

At that moment, Kandick's thick skull surfaced above the edge of the dune.

Your brother stood up to return to his hut because he wished to avoid rebuking Kandick for the
five hundredth time for oversleeping.

I felt happy.

Until that evening we had no further conversation. I took over the phone while he and Kandick went
on duty. That meant he went from one emplacement
to the next, attended drill, while Kandick, on the alert
for any possible injury during weapons practice,
slept near the latrine—a portable outhouse standing
somewhat higher up.

At eleven a.m. Kandick relieved me again; I had
to go to company headquarters before they went off
duty. In Pochelet—the hamlet where the orderly
room was—I was handed instructions to go to battalion headquarters where I was to be interrogated
by a judicial officer about an incident that had taken
place while I was still in Paris. I gulped down my
meal in order to reach Crutelles punctually by twelve-
thirty. Fortunately the sun wasn't shining. While
pedaling at top speed past that lonely tavern, I cast
a desperate glance into the empty garden.

The interrogation took place in a small room at
battalion headquarters, conducted by a bilious second
lieutenant who was a law graduate and due to be pro-
moted to lieutenant in our regiment.

I had to watch my step very closely. I was supposed to give evidence about a comrade at my Paris headquarters who, as transpired during the liquidation of the unit, had for years been trading in blank forms for French identity documents. How much money had he spent, how many women had he had, and what purchases had he made; had anything aroused my suspicions? In answering all these questions with a quaking conscience, I tried to spare the accused as much as possible, feigning ignorance. Actually I was in extreme danger myself. I, too, had forged documents in order to acquire cigarettes; I had placed horse-racing bets and won, and in dingy bars I had exchanged German money for French.

For almost an hour he squeezed me from every angle, but each time I sidestepped skillfully into the inviolable naïveté of a simple mind, with the result that he got nothing out of me. He had to let me go.

"Damn it," he muttered through his teeth, "it's like wading through mud; you just don't get anywhere."

I rode back very slowly; by this time it was almost two o'clock. Three days earlier I had come past that tavern at almost the same hour. I dismounted, threw the bike against the house wall, and tried the door. It was locked.

I was aghast. Hadn't she said: I'm always here?

But then, what does "always" mean? What do all

those words mean that we utter so thoughtlessly? I rattled the doorknob, shouted—no reaction. I walked around the house, climbed over a small locked gate into the yard, rattled all the doorknobs, walked into the stable, stared into the calm eyes of the cows. I called and called—there was no one about. I climbed back over the gate, walked around the entire property, but there was nothing to be seen except for those sweltering meadows with their reed-choked rivulets . . . a few sleepy cows . . . not a living soul. . . .

When would I have another chance to get out of the mousetrap? When would circumstances ever be so favorable again? Already I was making plans to sneak off at night or to invent stories that would justify another trip to battalion headquarters. My God, I simply *had* to see her!

In a fit of jealousy I hated every stone of that bumpy courtyard where, within half an hour, her feet might be treading again; full of jealousy I hated the doorknobs she would touch with her hands that smelled of milk. I hated the whole house, and that fierce hatred was almost identical with the hope of seeing her again. The hope of the flesh is despair.

While I desperately pedaled off on my bicycle, I concocted an infallible plan for seeing her again. Our plans are always infallible. I would report sick, then I would have to go to battalion headquarters, and once I was in Crutelles, there would be nothing to stop me from seeing her again.

But there was something else in store for me.

▲5▲

I BEGAN BY deciding to get drunk at Cadette's.

Just as the *ultima ratio* of the Christian is prayer, so my last resort was drink.

Any kind of narcotic holds an irresistible attraction for me. Maybe I should have become a chemist, providing mankind with new drugs of oblivion, though I know I'd never have had the will-power to study the subject in depth and face possible failures in my experiments; I am not only weak, I am also impatient. Everything has to happen immediately: I couldn't wait to see that girl and put my arms around her. . . .

Every soldier demands the solace of instant forgetfulness. Let this be your explanation for the apparently inexplicable and, for civilians, shockingly direct link between soldiers and prostitutes. The prostitute supplies instant gratification.

Every soldier permanently faces death, swaying on a gently teetering or perilously bouncing springboard that is ready to hurl him off.

While I was cycling back, the certainty that I
would never see her again filled me with true despair. Never again to see that pale face, never again
those compelling eyes and that darkly gleaming au-
burn hair above the pale olive skin. . . .

I decided to get drunk at Cadette's.

A soldier's good-bye is always, as it were, a good-
bye forever. Think of that massive, insane load of
pain hauled across Europe by those leave-trains! Oh,
if only those filthy corridors could speak, those grimy
windowpanes scream! If only those railway stations,
those ghastly railway stations—if only they would at
last cry out with the pain and despair they have seen!
There would be no more war. But with twenty pails
of whitewash one of those terrible railway halls has
been restored to a forum for cheerful idiots: six
brushes and a few raptly whistling painters on scaf-
folding, and life goes on. Life goes on. People go on
living because of their weak memory. They walk
through the same barrier through which they once
passed full of the fear of death; but today, only a few
years later, they are laughing, on their way to help
in the erection of some Potemkin façade.

Oh, if only the fallen could speak, those who were
hauled away in some train or other to their death,
their faces gray and sad, their pockets full of jam
sandwiches. If the dead could speak, there would be
no more war. But look at me: the only survivors are

the glib ones, those who weasled their way through, who were smart; there wasn't a trap in Europe that could catch them.

Oh, if only there were nothing but infantrymen, all that shouting about war or no war would be superfluous. There would be no more war. All those surviving heroes, those specialists for whom war was a game, a game that had the attraction of being a little bit risky: all those glib ones praise war and, in the boredom of their bourgeois monotony, long for the "good old days." . . . Oh, if only there were nothing but infantrymen! There used to be no need to spell out that war was despicable. Everyone knew it was gruesome, a pestilence, a horror. Just take a look today at those sentimental idiots stretching out their fancy little boots under the desks in their boring offices.

Oh, to get drunk, drunk . . .

I finished two bottles before that terrible mollusc face behind the bar ceased to disgust me. Only then did my loosened tongue give me the courage to tell her straight out that even her sweetest of sweet smiles would not seduce me. She confined herself to bringing me more bottles, carefully sorting out my butts, and sometimes throwing in a good-natured word of comfort that I couldn't take amiss.

I daresay you don't know that strange feeling of sitting on a bar stool and realizing one's consciousness is gradually growing confused. There one sits, without moving, staring into space, yet filled with adventurous life. This vibrating immobility of the drunk can only be compared to the contained confidence of a tightrope walker, swinging high up between two towers in infinity. If one were to see that man only as far down as his feet, one would think, What a cautious fellow, how slowly and cautiously he is walking! Yet in reality the man on the tightrope is being quite *un*cautious.

The secret of blissful drunkenness is a balanced imbalance.

Take this paradox any way you like. One pours wine into one's mouth, feels it pass the critical gateway of the palate, and at first everything flows into a silent underground reservoir that must be filled—until suddenly a kind of barometer starts to rise. Invisibly and quite involuntarily, something takes shape that resembles a U-shaped tube connecting the mind to the body, happiness and well-being increase as the levels of both sides of the tube approach each other. Body and mind are brought into balance—it is a constant interplay—like tightrope walking . . . an exquisite test of one's own equilibrium. Incredibly clear insights transfix one but leave nothing behind. How sad! But no doubt their lack of substance corresponds to their indeterminate origin.

I was also perfectly aware that Cadette was cheating me (all publicans live off drunks). Several

times, after wiping away the figure indicating the
bottles I had consumed, she wrote down a higher one.
I said nothing. Part of that condition is a sublime sense
of total indifference to material things. There is no
doubt that love and drunkenness, even under the most
sordid circumstances, have something sublime about
them even in their final stages. So I let Cadette do
as she pleased, partly because of that indifference but
also from inertia. I couldn't be bothered to open my
mouth merely to start a conversation, let alone an
argument, with that repulsive mask. She watched me
tensely, like a spider lying in wait for the fly's last
drop of blood. . . .

Later one never remembers how one got home.
Yet, with that deadly accuracy known only to the
drunk, one has taken the safest and most direct route
back.

Naturally the body has its revenge by allowing the
barometer of well-being to drop far below zero. Four
hours of sleep would have been enough for me, but
Kandick was nothing if not petty. I had telephone
duty, and I had to sit it out, even though he spent the
next two hours slumped beside me. There he sat, laboriously scrawling a letter to his wife, now and then
giving me a gloating poke in the ribs. Those fellows
see to it that regulations are complied with!

Your brother had gone off to a staff meeting. He
did not return, as I later found out, until almost eight

o'clock, by which time I was asleep and Kandick had
gone to bed. Your brother then sat beside me from
eight until nearly midnight. I slept like a dead man;
not even the shrill ringing of the phone right beside
my ear wakened me. Sleep after wine is almost as
delicious as the wine itself: that sinking into a blue
well, into bottomless depths, with a wistful fear in
one's heart, until one has sunk all the way down into
a sediment of dark semi-consciousness. The man
drunk on wine unconsciously performs strange em-
bryonic gestures in his sleep; it is like a thrusting
against the womb, and the awakening is like a birth:
pain coupled with bliss. . . . I seemed to be clinging
firmly to something, something that I wanted to pull
toward me, but now it was pulling me. When I awoke,
I found myself looking into your brother's smiling
face and holding one of his tunic buttons in my hand.

Well, of course it was embarrassing; I didn't
know where to look, but he caught my eye and asked:
"Is your head reasonably clear?"

"Completely," I said, and it really was.

He stood up and looked over to the bunk where
Kandick was sleeping, gently snoring. Sitting down
again he began in a low voice: "Listen, I implore you:
don't drink! If you start drinking you'll be done for.
If after only three days you need this phony, short-
lived consolation, you'll be finished in a month. Find
your consolation in staying sober, I beg you." He fell

silent. Because of the blackout, the window had to be kept closed, the door too; the air smelled stale. An uncanny silence hung heavily over the room. I stood up, turned off the light without asking, and opened door and window: a breath of mild, cool air came in, free and fresh.

"Hell," he continued, "I hate lecturing anyone. It reeks of moralism, and, no matter what, there's always that holier-than-thou echo: I'm different—me, *I'm* not like that—look at me! I implore you, come to your senses." Then he suddenly asked, his tone vehement and brusque, "What are you looking for in booze?" Startled, I had to search for words, and the only thing I could think of was the threadbare platitude: "Oblivion and happiness."

"Happiness?" he repeated. "Happiness? We weren't born to be happy. We were born to suffer, and to know why we suffer. Our suffering is the only thing we will have to show for our lives. Good deeds can be performed only by a few saints, not by us . . . and as for prayer . . . perhaps you don't understand that—or perhaps better than I . . . do you?" I was silent. Something prevented me from telling him about the girl; besides, this was my first experience of such melodramatic statements, and I was taken aback. I could only long for dawn never to come again.

"And if you can't understand that we weren't born to be happy, you will at least understand that we weren't born to forget. Oblivion and happiness! We were born to remember. Not to forget but to remember—that's what we're here for."

He spoke in a very low voice, but rarely have words had such an unforgettable impact on me. Kandick was asleep; outside in the dark the tide was rolling back, down the barely perceptible slope of the beach.

I couldn't think of any reply.

"You won't drop off again now, will you?" he finally asked quietly.

"I won't," I said.

"Good night."

"Good night."

He stood up, cautiously opened the door to his room, and I was alone. Quietly and steadily the tide rolled back, quietly and imperturbably Kandick went on snoring.

My first thought, after your brother had closed the door behind him, was: I will see her again! I can't forget that. . . .

Every awakening was terrible, sir. Any consolation one imagined to have been gained the previous night had dissolved in the light of day, and none of the ocean's beauty, no freshness of wind or quiet gurgling of water, was of any help.

Several days passed in a strange uneasy calm. I performed my duties methodically, and time went on like an unchanging ribbon drawn across a turbulent background. Whenever I was on telephone duty in the evening, your brother would sit beside me. Kandick had started operating a canteen in the cellar of a dynamited house behind the dunes.

In our conversations we never mentioned a name, never identified by name or title an institution or person of that foundering Reich. We played games with the language, we were like two kids playing ball, bouncing it—depending on energy or mood—fourteen times or seven times against the wall and, the moment we felt our strength giving out, quickly returning the ball to our playmate.

"Any person," your brother might say, "who is incapable of recognizing his own inadequacy is a nincompoop and essentially stupid. A vain genius is no longer a genius. Anyone who isn't aware that he is part of an unknown plan is stupid. There is no such thing as a stupid genius—ergo, he's no longer a genius. Which only leaves the inglorious possibility of being a genius of stupidity—or of crime. Do you follow me?"

"I do," I said, "and think of a blockhead who considers himself a genius, and every day he is confirmed in this by the hoarse roaring of the crowds— say eighty million—confirming that he is a genius, and a universal genius at that: artist, statesman, strategist—all to an unprecedented degree. Every day they roar that at him. He is perfection personified. Anyone attempting to claim, for instance, 'I am like X,' would be avenged more drastically than if he were to say, 'I am like God.' Don't you agree?"

"Of course. To demand that such a person come to his senses is almost impossible. But how to render him harmless?"

"There's only one way," I said. "He must be assassinated."

"O.K. Assassinated. But then come the problems. How to get at him, what route to choose? You see. . . ."

For several days that was how we discussed all the institutions of that damnable regime, reducing them to zero, blowing them up like soap bubbles, letting them collapse again, then gathering up all that was left to have a good look at whatever remained of substance.

In this way a few days passed quickly enough. One evening about five I had, as usual, ridden off to company headquarters. It was always a relief to get out of the mousetrap. I cycled slowly along that wonderful avenue leading from the beach, between the mined houses, past Cadette's tavern and onto the highway. I was always glad to see people—women, civilians. My God, the pleasure the sight of a woman can give a soldier, when he spends all his time with men, with men only, their smell, their garrulousness, their dirt, all their dry gruffness. I always looked forward to those trips. And how lucky I was compared to all those others who, if they were lucky, were allowed to leave the base once a month. Of course, escapes were dreamed up with a recklessness explicable only by a desperate longing for the world: secret paths through the minefields, sudden desertion of one's post, but for most of them that world existed only in Cadette's dubious consolations.

So I always took my time, maybe stopping for a beer or a glass of wine on the way, picking up mail and passwords in the orderly room, and pedaling back just as leisurely.

By now it was September; the heat hadn't abated very much. In the evenings it lay like sultry clouds on the sandy patches among the pine groves. A hot, stifling monotony pervaded the huts, most of them being wooden barracks that soaked up the heat.

That day the company commander was in a good mood. Normally he would keep pestering me about petty details: the shine on my boots or belt, the cleanliness of my bicycle. That he was in a good mood was something I noticed as soon as I came in. His eyes were shining. I was soon to learn the cause. Beautifully shaven, tanned, he was wearing a light summer tunic and carelessly flapping his cap at the flies drumming on the windowpanes of the orderly room. The

topkick seemed ill at ease; the orderly was wearing
his expression of Olympian indifference. That fellow
Schmidt could express everything by way of indifference: contempt, friendship, pleasure, hatred.

"I leave it to you, Fischer my friend, to see how
you manage it. In any event, it's time something was
done to improve the company's food supplies. The
ground has been laid, the practical details are up to
you. Heil Hitler! I'm looking forward to that roast!"

As he walked past me, I flung open the door and
stood at attention. Before leaving the room he paused
and said to me: "I'm very satisfied with you—a
pleasant surprise, I must say!" I almost bowed before that handsome schoolmaster. He stalked out: a
fine figure of a man, endowed with everything—good
looks, a splendid physique, and all the decorations
appropriate to evening wear neatly displayed on his
chest.

"Goddamn it," exclaimed the topkick, throwing
down his pen. "When he smells food there's no holding him."

The orderly laughed: "He says the calf's brain is
for him, he's been hoping for some for quite a while."

"I'd rather see the brain of an old sow in his
belly," cried the topkick. Then he looked at me, and,
his eyes lighting up, he exclaimed: "Say! You can
speak French, can't you?"

"Yes," I said.

"Can you handle cattle?"

"No."

He laughed. "Never mind. Listen: tonight at 0200 hours we're supposed to fetch a cow from a farmer two kilometers from here—d'you think you can manage that?"

I shrugged. "If I can have a horse and cart, some money, and two men to help."

"Done!" cried the topkick. "And the next Cross of Merit to be handed out in this bunch is yours."

He took the map out of the drawer; I bent over his desk and asked him to show me the place. It was a tiny hamlet, two kilometers northeast toward the Somme. I was to meet the cart at the crossroads at 0200 hours, but I was also to ride over there this evening to give the farmer exact instructions. I was delighted with the assignment. Any opportunity to taste a little unscheduled freedom was more than welcome. Besides, I thought it might lead me to a cheap source of butter, for Cadette charged exorbitant prices for everything, and my money was slowly running out.

▲6▲

Your brother was also in very good spirits that evening. During the briefing he had hinted that there was shortly to be some addition to the rations. As we went back to the bunker, I asked him: "So you know about it?" I imagined he had been referring to the scheme to buy a cow.

"No," he said in surprise. I explained my assignment. He was delighted: "Why, that's terrific! Then you'll have no trouble carrying out my plan at the same time. I was thinking of buying a sheep for our base."

I had planned to leave as soon as possible, but first there was a meeting I had to attend. We had come to the conclusion that, by extending the sentry's time on duty by only half an hour every night, we could ensure that each man on the base would get one night of unbroken sleep at least once every two weeks. With a garrison of twenty-eight men, this amounted to a gain of fourteen hours' extra sleep per day: i.e., for each man one night without sentry duty. I had volunteered to draw up the schedule; since we had to note down the individual sentries at each strongpoint every night in a sentry log, we were familiar with the technique of devising a sentry schedule. A meeting of all

the N.C.O.'s—three corporals and a lance corporal—
had been called; they brought along the results of a
poll taken among their men: the plan had been re-
jected—the men suspected duplicity. In particular, a
certain Töpfer, one of the older soldiers in the lance
corporal's group, had asked what would happen if
someone were suddenly transferred: if he had been
doing his extra half hour for a number of days, who
was going to make up for his lost sleep to him?

Your brother listened calmly, then shrugged his
shoulders: "Obviously I can't force anybody. But try
to explain to the men that, no matter what, *we*
wouldn't benefit at all. Maybe then they'll agree." He
looked at each of the four in turn. "Oh well, perhaps
the men are right. Sentry duty is as ancient as playing soldiers, and sentry hours are just as ancient. And
you can be sure that if it were possible to demand
more from a soldier under normal circumstances, it
would be demanded. Still, it might be worth a try."
He paused for a moment, then said: "O.K., nothing
doing, gentlemen. That'll be all. And you, Nolte,"
he said, turning to the youngest corporal, "please have
the gap in the mine fence repaired this evening, pref-
erably with old wire so it won't show, right?"

Nolte blushed; we all saluted and left.

I followed your brother into his room. He opened
the window, beckoned me to his side, and pointed
toward the south, where the beach was mined down

to the high-tide line—a broad stretch of coast reaching as far as the next company's sector. A wonderful, still intact children's summer camp was located there in a dense minefield close to the beach. Perhaps there had been a reluctance to blow it up because it was such a valuable piece of property. I looked in that direction but was taken aback by his question: "Haven't you noticed anything about the outgoing mail the last couple of days?"

"Yes," I said in surprise. "It contained a tremendous number of small parcels."

"Right!" he went on with a laugh. "All unawares, you have been transporting, bit by bit, that children's summer camp to Dresden, Leipzig, Glauchau, and Schneiwitzenmühl or wherever. That's right!" he said, in response to my look of amazement. "For the last few days Nolte's group has been systematically looting over there during their off-duty hours. Now Frieger's group has got into the act, and soon there's going to be a glorious free-for-all, and today or tomorrow the entire base will be sneaking through the dunes on stocking feet to make sure they're not being done out of their share."

"For God's sake!" I cried. "What about the mines?"

"That's the least of their worries, there's no danger there, although they might bump into each other. But Nolte, that ingenious fellow, has ferreted out a sapper corporal from the regiment at Geneu, a man who originally helped lay the mines so they have an accurate chart. Besides, mines that have had three years to rust through aren't that dangerous anymore. I only hope Nolte got the hint. Shortly before you arrived here, one of my corporals was court-martialed for snipping through mine fences with a wire cutter: the cows smelled the high, lush grass and naturally in they went. Result: two badly injured cows that had to be slaughtered on the spot." He gave another laugh. "Let's hope Nolte is sensible—I'd find it very difficult to report anything. The embarrassing thing is, you see, that I have nothing against looting."

He lit a cigarette, then slowly and happily blew the smoke out through the window; he seemed altogether very cheerful and relaxed that evening. "Listen," he said. "The way I feel, it's simply part of a soldier's job. One can't expect a soldier to behave like a chaplain on a summer vacation. Every occupation has its game rules. These laborers, shoemakers, electricians, they've been turned into soldiers, these good men have been made ferocious, proud, after having first been tamed. See what I mean?"

I saw nothing.

"O.K., then, let me explain. We stick these good men into uniform and destroy what the Prussians like to call gutlessness: a sense of human dignity and the glorious freedom of a civilian. O.K. So much for that. The barracks have—it is assumed—fulfilled their objective. Then the men are sent out to kill or get killed, and this activity makes them a bit wild, even here where there's no killing. And especially when these heroes don't get enough to eat. But then they are confronted with regulations that demand more tameness from them than from a civilian. More respectability, dignity, self-sacrifice than they have ever in their lives possessed. They are forbidden to loot while at the same time they are allowed to go hungry. There you have a typical German incongruity. They rant and rave in their speeches, they want to reform the world, they call that 'revolution,' yet they're so scared for their good reputation that they wet their pants when a few soldiers happen to smash some windowpanes and grab a sausage or a couple of shirts. Do you follow me?"

I could only nod, astonished at this new, reckless frankness.

"On we go, then!" he exclaimed. "I can't wait to get this off my chest. All right, you can't have a slaughterhouse without a lot of blood, and a person who can't stand that should stop eating meat. And looting is, in my opinion, the inalienable right of every soldier. The point is not that looting should be prohibited but that we shouldn't turn these men into soldiers. The whole idiotic nonsense begins with the ill-conceived romantic notion of a 'people's army.'

Damn it all, soldiering is a profession, and it can be learned. And if they are forced—and they *are* all forced, all these good men—we shouldn't be surprised if maybe they do turn into soldiers. Well," he said as he walked over to his bed, "I hope you take my hints to heart and manage the job in such a way that I don't see anything. Now, off you go, and don't forget that sheep."

I left and got onto my bike.

The map given me by the topkick proved reliable. Beyond the crossing that led to the orderly room, I had to continue straight ahead for some distance and then make a right turn. Here some of the paths were already dangerous. They led past swampy patches sweltering away in the heat, saturated with silence. Twice I crossed a little stream, and after five minutes' pedaling I admit I felt a certain uneasiness at not having seen the slightest sign of human habitation. But immediately after passing a clump of trees I saw a solitary house. The way I read the map, that must be the spot marked "Daval." Almost every farmhouse in the world is entered from the rear, and as I turned into the yard I saw a very peaceful scene: a dark-haired woman sitting with a basket in front of her, shelling peas, a youth of about fourteen helping her, and the farmer sitting beside them smoking his pipe. I had interrupted their chat. Their laughter died away when I silently rounded the corner and stopped on the sandy ground. The woman let out a little scream, the man turned toward me without a word, and the youth looked curiously at the insignia on my sleeve.

"Good evening," I said. "Excuse me, but is this Daval?"

They exchanged glances. I had the impression they were expecting a confiscation or something of the kind, so I said: "I have to get to Tulby."

"Over there," said the man, pointing his pipe in an easterly direction.

"Is this Daval then?"

"Yes," he said curtly.

"Do you know Monsieur Preter?"

"Yes," came the curt reply again, "he's her uncle." He pointed his pipe at his wife.

"Oh, I see," I said.

The woman glanced up briefly, and she struck me as being less hostile than the man. The farmer stared at me unabashedly. "Monsieur," I said to him, "couldn't you sell us a sheep?"

"Who wants to buy?" he asked frostily.

I tried to explain and mentioned a price of about thirty marks.

The husband and wife exchanged smiles; then the man said: "I suppose you mean twice that much, if— and I say, if," he drawled, "*if* I were to sell one."

"Perhaps we could talk about it."

"This year," he said shortly, "the weather's been

too dry. I can't sell you a sheep. Not enough fodder for the animals."

"All the more reason," I said.

"What do you mean?"

"Well, if you haven't enough fodder, we'll slaughter one, and you'll have one less mouth to feed."

He laughed, no longer quite so hostile.

I felt like sitting down with them and helping with the peas; it was a wonderful evening, but standing there in that hated uniform, leaning on the crossbar of my bike, my cap in my hand, I felt very homeless.

"Well, what about it?" I asked.

"You're a very stubborn fellow."

"We're hungry."

His apathetic eyes lit up a bit. "You're hungry?" he asked, almost like a child. "Doesn't your company feed you, then?"

I was genuinely ashamed and blushed.

"O.K.," I said impatiently, "yes or no?"

"Claire"—he turned toward his wife—"what do you think?"

I knew I had won. The woman hesitated, without looking up: "At that price . . . ," she said.

He stood up. "Follow me."

We went into the house.

I struck a deal with him and agreed that we would come for the sheep that night. I left the equivalent

of forty-five marks in francs with him. It was hard
to leave the house. I stood there for a while after
coming back from the stable, slowly finished my cigarette, and looked at the sky as it hung, a soft and rosy
gray, over the sea. It was very quiet, there was only
the distant croaking of frogs and the soft, almost
musical sound of the peas as they hopped out of their
shells into the tin bowl and sometimes bounced off the
edge with a light ping.

I was also aware of the gentle hiss of the man's
pipe as he sucked on it; and, although that icy hostility between us had been replaced by a certain
goodwill, I could feel that I was not only intruding
but unwelcome.

So I threw my butt onto the flagstones, hastily
ground it out, said "Good night," and got back onto
my bike. I soon reached the neighboring farm situ-
ated in a dense little wood, one of those silent, dilapidated places often to be found thereabouts. The
terrible part about those farms is that they look deserted whereas there are actually people living in
them. What's missing is something of the atmosphere
that is part and parcel of rural life: everything is
pervaded by a kind of idleness that to us seems totally
unrural, an air of decadence, of almost literary melancholy that, in the context of a farm, seems quite
horrifying.

The farmer and his wife were sitting in the dark kitchen, and the first thing I saw was the glow of a cigarette.

"Good evening," I said, instinctively keeping my voice low. "I've come about the cow."

"Cow?" a woman's voice repeated slowly and sarcastically.

"That's right," a man's hoarse voice replied, equally sarcastically, more to the woman than to me. "They want to buy a cow, but . . ."

"I thought the deal was all settled," I broke in.

"Settled!" repeated that disagreeable male voice; I couldn't make out the face that went with it. "Nothing is settled, *nothing* has been settled, d'you get me?"

I was silent.

Since nobody offered me a chair, I sat down on a stool by the window and began to smoke.

"Settled!" resumed that voice, this time a little less confidently.

"I was told," I remarked, "that the purchase had been completed. The cow's supposed to be picked up tonight."

"*Merde!*" shouted the voice. "That's what I'd call rushing things! Nothing doing—in Paris people are paying fifty francs for a kilo of meat, and you expect me to sell four hundred kilos for five thousand francs! I'm not crazy, not by a long shot. . . ."

"All right," I said evenly. "Put a rope around

your cow's neck and take it to Paris. There you might even get eighty francs a kilo."

I could tell that the couple had both lifted their heads and were looking at me, but what bothered me was that I could see nothing except a pair of flashing knitting needles and the suggestion of a pale cloth cap; the cigarette had been spat out.

"After all," I said quietly, "nobody's forcing you to sell the cow, are they?"

The answer was a hostile silence.

These deals were a kind of legal black market, an infringement of a law that we had instituted ourselves and whose enforcement we should really have been safeguarding; but, as I already told you, soldiers who are permanently hungry don't give a damn about such laws. Needless to say, my question was ridiculous, since I was putting it as the delegate of an enemy company, even though, legally speaking, it was the farmer's duty to refuse the deal.

"No," came the sarcastic voice, "nobody's ever forced us, no indeed."

"Very well," I said as I stood up. "We'll be here tonight at two o'clock, I have part of the money with me." I opened my wallet and took from it three crisp, brand-new thousand-franc bills.

"Here you are," I said curtly.

There are few farmers who can resist the sight of real money. The couple were on their feet in a flash, the woman rushed to the light switch and turned it on. Now for the first time I could see them both, and immediately saw how they leaned their heads toward the money. They were old, gray-haired, with pinched faces, and for a moment I thought they were brother and sister, then I saw their worn wedding rings. The man couldn't resist; he took the bills from my hand and with a repulsive tenderness snapped them between his fingers.

We soldiers, sir, have a terrible contempt for money. Money alone is nothing. Its only value is what one can get for it at any given moment: wine, women, or tobacco. Money is no more than a means. To save it or hoard it seems to us absurd.

The deal was closed. The woman also offered me some butter and eggs; I left the house with a pound of butter, ten eggs, and a very special acquisition: a bottle of thick cream.

It was almost dark outside; a shadowy gloom hung over the meadows and bushes. Cautiously I rode back.

I was filled with a weary disgust. With complete clarity I could see everything that lay ahead: I would reach the highway, have a beer at Cadette's, then sit for four hours at the phone fighting sleep. I would smoke, although nothing tasted good; try to write a letter, without success; hear Kandick's snoring. And after two hours I would be left with nothing but fatigue, hopeless fatigue, and I would keep looking at my watch to see whether it wasn't time to waken Kandick. That's how it would be for the next four or five weeks; then we would be relieved, and in some godforsaken little place ten kilometers from the coast we would be drilled. I wouldn't even have any money left for booze, I'd have nothing to smoke, and after those six weeks I would once again be sitting in some other bunker night after night, at that phone that never rang, waiting for the moment when I would be allowed to sink into a leaden sleep.

At two a.m. I would be collecting the cow and the sheep, then sitting at the phone again from seven to eleven, riding off to company headquarters at eleven. . . .

I dismounted for a moment because the sound of the bicycle was getting on my nerves.

In those days, sir, I still believed in what is known as coincidence. I believed that our life was an isolated fragment surrounded by other isolated fragments, each a distinct and a more or less brilliant painting; I believed in the total lack of connection between all things and in the pale, blind futility of our existence; I had as yet no inkling of that mysterious network of innumerable knotted threads, of that vast, all-encompassing fabric into which for each one of us a particular thread has been woven. I reached the highway, got back on my bike, and rode off toward Cadette's tavern.

On opening the door I was assailed by an unaccustomed racket. Raucous singing and caterwauling. I caught sight of naval and air force uniforms—near our base there were a lighthouse and an air force listening post—and the next moment I was surrounded by soldiers who directed my attention to a figure sitting slumped on a bench by the window—glassy-eyed, unseeing, and mumbling incoherent, drunken nonsense. He was from our base, a man called Wiering, normally a quite inconspicuous person who, as far as I could recall the schedule, was nowhere near due for time off. I remembered that he had been due only a few days ago and that he had sold his leave for half a packet of tobacco. I took charge of Wiering, who, without even staggering overmuch, unresistingly let himself be led away. Cadette protested her innocence and accused a few laughing antiaircraft gunners of having made him drunk.

I handed Wiering over to his squad leader, and we agreed to try and say nothing about his absence. Then I entered the bunker, reported my success to your brother, and sat down resignedly at the phone. Kandick had risen from his chair as I came in, then sunk back on his bed; he was already snoring.

I declined your brother's offer to stay awake in my place and for a while sat silently across from him.

My silence contained a good deal of hostility. I hated that life, and I was transferring my hatred to your brother as the wearer of a uniform, the possessor of a rank that seemed to justify that life.

Finally he rose, went toward his room, turned at the door, and said: "Don't forget that our lives can change at any minute. Nothing is unalterable. Good night." Perhaps he already knew that his words were soon to come true.

▲7▲

Events now followed in such rapid succession that I must first sort them out in my memory if I am to keep them in the right order.

That night I had almost no sleep. Fatigue and despair filled me like an ever-recurring, evil-tasting tide that I had to keep regurgitating; back and forth it flooded, unwilling either to retreat or to utterly engulf me.

Just before two I was wakened by Kandick, who had relieved me at midnight, and I rode off to meet the cook and collect the cow and the sheep: an arduous enterprise accompanied by much frustration and cursing.

It was close to five when, totally exhausted, I was

able to start on my way back, and the sky was already growing light as I turned into the avenue at Cadette's tavern. A glorious morning no doubt, but I was too tired to notice; how pointless and totally irrelevant that grayish-pink light seemed to me as it felt its way up the gray vault of the night sky with delicate, soft rays. There is a stage of fatigue—what soldier is not familiar with it!—that is almost deadly to body and soul. One would commit murder for a single night of unbroken sleep; one is on the verge of tears from exhaustion, indifferent to everything except sleep or oblivion.

When I stepped inside the bunker, Kandick was asleep, sprawled across the table. Even my noisy entrance failed to wake him. I simply flung myself down on my bunk and instantly fell asleep, too tired even to give Kandick a poke in the ribs; besides, I was beyond caring what happened. As far as I was concerned, anybody who liked could come and capture our base.

When I awoke it was midday: a steaming mess kit was on the table. Your brother was sitting beside it, calmly looking at me. He was about to open his mouth to say something to me when the phone rang. He lifted the receiver, spoke, and the next moment I saw an expression of utter astonishment on his face. Then he repeated several times: "Yes, I understand, yes. . . ." He put down the receiver and burst out laughing.

What had happened was this: our C.O. had ordered the brain of the cow that had been slaughtered that night to be fried for himself at around eleven a.m., had polished it off, and then suddenly been taken so violently ill that it had been necessary to rush him to the field hospital in Abbeville. (Incidentally, on account of chronic dyspepsia he was considered "unfit for service on the Eastern Front.") Your brother, being next in seniority, was put in command of the company.

Within an hour your brother and I had to move from Larnton to Pochelet. With our scanty baggage we settled into the C.O.'s quarters, a nice little four-room house, and for the time being were happy to have escaped from Larnton. Two more hours were enough to make ourselves reasonably comfortable in our new quarters and to remove the baggage of the former C.O. At four o'clock your brother went over to the orderly room to take charge.

I spent the whole afternoon sitting on our little terrace with a view of the sea, reading the Kierke-gaard diaries your brother had lent me.

Since by eight o'clock he hadn't returned, I went to bed and fell asleep at once. I was worn out by the exertions of the previous night and of the day, and the prospect of sleeping the whole night through without interruption seemed irresistible.

The next morning I slept in until nearly eight. I barely had time to wake your brother before hurrying off to the drill in which I now had to take part. For the first time in three years I had to endure the ordeal of foot drill. You can't imagine the horror I feel to this day at having merely to write the words "position of attention," those words that form the very foundation of Prussian drill procedure.

At about eight-thirty your brother drove off to take over the command of two bases farther north.

The morning dragged slowly on. At noon I was alone. I listlessly ate my meal, then dozed on my bunk, smoking cigarettes and drinking half a bottle of wine.

Your brother's return awakened me; I heard him come in, go to his room, throw down his belt. Shortly after that he called me in.

He seemed tired and put out and at once asked me for a cigarette. We sat facing each other in armchairs, and after a few puffs he surprised me by pulling out a bottle of wine from under the table. He took two glasses from a cupboard, opened the bottle, and poured. We touched glasses and drank.

"Listen," he said finally, after we had sat in silence for a few minutes. "There are people who are born to polish boots. A perfectly unobjectionable, dignified occupation. Perhaps you were not born for that, I don't know. On the other hand, I don't want anyone else around me but you. I think we will be able to talk in greater privacy and at greater length and less in innuendoes. Because I want to *do* something, understand? Not only talk. We have to do something, understand?"

I nodded, although I wasn't very clear about what he meant.

"So," he went on, "it'll be best if we share the boot polishing. Right? One day I do yours and mine, the next you do yours and mine. Is that a deal? Apart from that, you will be on duty in the mornings and have the afternoons off, to which a C.O.'s orderly is entitled. We won't infringe on any regulations. And there's another thing you'll have to take over, something I simply can't do: the cooking."

I gave him a long look. "I have a counter-proposal," I said. "Each of us will polish his own boots. I'll be glad to do the cooking and collect our rations."

"Splendid," he cried, "splendid! A good idea. Thanks very much." He shook my hand, raised his glass to me, I raised mine to him. Then he suddenly stood up, walked toward the big portrait of Hitler that hung on the end wall of the room—an ostentatious affair in a heavy gilt frame—and without a word turned it back to front. His hand was still on the frame when the door opened and Schnecker stood on the threshold.

I jumped to my feet, as stipulated: Schnecker looked first at me, then at your brother, who had meanwhile moved back to the table. Then Schnecker said to me in a low voice: "Leave us, please."

I walked to the door, saluted, and left the room.

With heavy steps I walked along the corridor, listening intently, but there was nothing to be heard yet, and I supposed he was waiting for my footsteps to die away. I left the house, but walked around to the rear and lay down in the garden under the open window. There was still no sound.

"Well, then," Captain Schnecker finally said in a calm voice—he had apparently gone over to the wall and turned the picture back to its proper position—"let's begin by correcting this childishness."

"May I ask you," said your brother, his voice just as calm, "whether this is my own living room and whether there is any regulation requiring officers to have portraits of the Führer in their home?"

"No."

I could hear your brother walking over to the wall, and I knew he was turning the picture around again.

"Good," said the captain, "excellent. But with

your indisputable intelligence it must be clear to you that there is not much room for doubt when in the presence of his subordinate an officer displays loathing for the portrait of his supreme commander."

"Wrong, my friend. All I loathe is the frame. You know quite well how sensitive I am when it comes to art, and to me it is outright blasphemy to frame the portrait of our modest, simple, soldierly Führer— who has said he won't take off his soldier's tunic as long as the war lasts—to stick his portrait in such a garish frame: to me that's an insult to his person. And after all, the Führer is also an artist."

"You're as strong as ever in syntax, it seems."

"Stronger, I hope. I've had plenty of time to practice. You fellows saw to that."

They both fell silent, and I knew that your brother was standing there, his hands clasped behind his back, calmly looking Schnecker in the eye.

"Listen to me carefully," Schnecker resumed. "I have been at great pains to clear your name with the regiment and to see that the old affair is forgotten and you're put in command here. That sissy-pants will probably be spending six months in the hospital again and then go on leave and arrive back here with a brand-new stomach ulcer. There were some nasty types who would have liked to see you take orders from a junior lieutenant. I prevented that."

"I wouldn't have cared."

"Why do you think I did that for you?"

"To set a trap for me."

The captain gave a devilish laugh: "There couldn't have been any better trap for you than the mousetrap of Larnton! You could have grown old there. But no"—he raised his voice—"you can't think of anything better to do, on the very first day, the *very* first day, than to send in almost word for word the same report that was the original reason for your being found unfit to command a company. You can think of nothing better to do than worry about margarine, bread, and sugar for your men. It really does look as if you were out to create difficulties."

"I can't think of anything more important here than the bread, margarine, and sugar for my men. Unfortunately I cannot improve the fortifications at my own expense. That would probably be the next priority."

"You are simply making yourself ridiculous. And furthermore: on the very first day another of your requests to be transferred to Russia. Don't worry— the Russian Front still needs so many officers that your turn will come."

"What are you going to do with my report about the rations?" your brother asked quietly.

"I shall tear it up."

"No, you won't!" your brother shouted, and I could hear them moving toward each other.

"Then I'll wipe my ass with it!" shouted the captain furiously. "Here"—there was a brief pause—"here," he cried again, "look at this, read this scrap of paper. It was found yesterday on a carrier pigeon shot down in the sector of our first company. 'The morale of the troops is bad, and the troops are hungry.' Needless to say, it is extremely flattering for me as battalion commander, in the eyes of the regiment and the division, when a carrier pigeon that must have been released in my sector bears a message of that kind. That is indeed extremely flattering, and on top of that you also produce your idiotic report that"—he gave his voice a sarcastic undertone and was obviously quoting—"that the troops believe they are constantly being done out of small but regular quantities of fat, sugar, and bread; that the quartermaster-sergeants declared that, on the basis of the quantities they received, they were simply unable to issue the prescribed rations; and that"—his voice became shrill—"that this naturally served further to deteriorate the low morale of the quartermaster-sergeants, for where there was an actual shortage of two grams it was easy enough to pilfer five grams. Oh, all that's just great for me!"

"The question is whether it's untrue." Your brother's voice was calm again.

"Untrue! We're not here to seek the truth, which anyway doesn't exist—we're here to win the war."

"And apparently that can only be done by constantly gypping hungry soldiers, right?"

This was followed by a terrible silence, and they must have moved even closer together.

"I daresay you believe," came Schnecker's hoarse voice at last, "that I am eating your men's margarine and sugar myself, do you?"

Your brother said nothing.

"Do you believe that? I said: Do you believe that?" His voice seemed to be exploding with rage.

"Not directly, of course."

"Indirectly then, right?"

"Now you listen to me." Your brother's voice was very calm. "This paymaster is not only a fool, he's also a bastard. You wouldn't deny that?"

"Of course not. But there's no way I can get rid of the fellow."

"You don't have to. You just have to make him watch his step. And you can't do that, of course, because you depend on him for your extra supplies of booze, to which, of course, you're not entitled either. You see, you need to get drunk every day. I know: on a captain's pay one can get good and drunk three times a month at the most, I know that too. And then, of course, you need women. You're a good-looking fellow, a ladies' man, as they say. There you are, then. There's no way you can get at the paymaster.

Those fellows are businessmen; in other words they've covered themselves in every possible direction. And you know I'm right, don't you?"

The terrible part was that I couldn't see anything, and now I couldn't hear anything either, and at that moment, lying out there under the windowsill, I realized that eavesdropping is horrible.

What was Schnecker doing, for God's sake? Was he sitting there slumped in his chair, or was he standing there, pistol in hand, ready to shoot your brother at any moment? I lay there as if dead, not daring to stir or crawl away. . . .

Again came your brother's voice, "You must try to see my point," he said. "I can't imagine anything worse than cheating a soldier out of his rations or his sleep. After all, we in our officer's uniforms represent the power that compels these men to submit to being killed or being bored to death. That burden is quite enough for me. I wouldn't like the added responsibility of making them suffer more hunger than is provided for by the system." He fell silent again; then after a while his voice continued, heavier and more somber than before. "In a way it's too bad that I'm going to die—otherwise I'd look forward to writing a philosophical treatise on the gram after the war."

Now I realized that Schnecker had been standing there grinning all the time, his arms folded. He burst into a peal of laughter, as if a pent-up flood were being released.

"Who would have believed it?" he said in a strong, firm voice. "And from the lips of someone wearing the uniform of a German officer! Who would have believed it?" Again that ringing laughter.

"Come now"—I could tell from his voice that he was tightening his belt and straightening up—"let's get back to business. For all I care, the report can go to regimental headquarters. For all I care, make yourself ridiculous, make yourself a laughing-stock for the sake of three grams of margarine, for the sake of three grams that *have* to be withheld. And another thing: did you have to pick the cheekiest bastard in the battalion for your orderly and sit here boozing with him in the afternoon while you were both still on duty?"

Your brother was evidently looking at him in silence; then he laughed: "Oh, of course," he said, "that's right—it was four-thirty when you arrived. I leave it to you to file a counter-report."

After hearing the captain get into his car, I crawled back into the shelter of some nearby bushes, stood up, and hurried off toward the forest that blocked the view of the sea. Leaning against the trunk of a fir

tree, I looked out over the waves as they rolled slowly
in. It was very quiet, the air was soft, and there was
nothing in sight but the water and the stretch of sand
in front of it that was slowly, very slowly being covered by the tide; the barbed wire that had been drawn
along the tide line was the only reminder of the war.

A painful sadness, such as I had never known
before, welled up in me. There is no justice, I thought,
there is no such thing as a gram. The gram is a fic-
tion, a gram is nothing, and yet they say: It is a gram!
And on this nothing, on this gram, they all grow rich.
They all grow rich solely on the gram, so it must be
something, that gram. That's why there have to be
so many poor, victimized people, because a gram is
so little and so many grams are needed to make a
rich man rich; that's why there have to be all those
millions of gray, gaunt figures obediently marching
across Europe with their rifles on their backs, just so
the rats can get fat on their only tasty food—the gram.
There must be vast numbers of those figures that can
be stuffed into a freight car designed to hold "40 soldiers or 8 horses"—simply because the horses are
bigger than the soldiers, bigger and more valuable.

I was twenty-five at the time, sir. I was no innocent, I was a trooper like all the rest; I believed in
nothing but the sausage on my bread, as we used to
say, in wine and tobacco. At least, I believed that was

all I believed. But where did that unutterable sadness
come from, weighing down my heart like lead, para-
lyzing me so that I felt too tired even to put my hand
in my pocket to dig out matches and cigarettes?

I had been fifteen when the swastika was sus-
pended like a huge black spider in the sky over Germany.

Now I wished I could travel across the sea, far,
far away to another world where there were no uniforms, no policemen, no war, but I was trapped in
this cage called Europe; there was no escape: starting from this coast I could travel eastward for thousands of kilometers, eastward to the end of this insane
continent, all the way to Vladivostok, and there would
be no life anywhere.

In that hour I would have sold all the rest of my
life to sink into the arms of that girl who had said,
I'm always here—and who hadn't been there after all.

As dusk fell I crept back home, lay down on my
bed, and abandoned myself to the sluggish tide of a
leaden despair that left no room even for desire. Not
a sound was to be heard in our cottage. From the barracks I could hear faint singing. I was incapable of
thinking or doing anything, I was at the end of my
tether.

▲8▲

Two days later we were already on our way to Russia.

When I woke up next morning, everything was normal. From the direction of the company kitchen I could hear the men whose job it was to take coffee to their barracks. In your brother's room all was quiet. It was seven o'clock, I got up, went into our own little kitchen, set the frying pan on the electric hotplate, put some fat in it, took the loaf of bread out of the drawer, and began to slice it. As the fat melted, I beat up the eggs in a cup with some cream and stirred them around in the pan. Then I prepared the tray, putting two plates, cups, and knives on it, and went off to the company kitchen.

The mornings were always peaceful. The whole little place had the atmosphere of a somewhat run-down summer camp. That morning the air was already warm, and the soldiers were standing outside their barracks, stripped to the waist and washing.

The topkick was sitting in the kitchen, discussing with the cook how to use up the rest of the cow. He was markedly cooler toward me.

"Please tell the C.O.," he called out to me while I was filling my mess tin at the coffee urn, "that church services have been scheduled for this afternoon, both denominations, here. The outposts have been notified."

"Yessir," I replied.

The cook also threw me a suspicious glance. He hadn't forgiven me for doing him out of his profit of five hundred francs on the cow, and he probably assumed I'd told your brother about it.

As I left the kitchen, Schmidt called across to me from the orderly room: "We need a dispatch runner for nine o'clock to pick up special orders from the battalion—would you be interested?"

I looked into Schmidt's placid, amiable face: "Yes," I said. All I could see was the pale face of the girl, and I imagined myself pressing my mouth onto her cheeks, her lips, and the little hollow at the base of her neck.

"Yes," I repeated.

As I approached our quarters I could already see your brother's face, covered with shaving soap, at the window. It was seven-thirty.

Shortly after that, I carried coffee, bread, and eggs into the room and told your brother about the church services and that I had been ordered for nine o'clock to ride over to battalion headquarters.

"Yes," he said as he put on his tunic. "There's something in the air, maybe the cow will be our farewell dinner."

"Do you really think so?" I asked doubtfully.

"Things look bad in Russia."

We sat down, I poured the coffee and we spread scrambled egg on the bread, but first I lit a cigarette. It was the first real breakfast in a long time. The wide, low window toward the north was open, the air, cool yet soft, streamed into the room, and one could see far out over the water.

Your brother, like me, picked up the bread and promptly put it down again, swallowed a mouthful of coffee, and suddenly began to speak in a rapid, almost droning voice:

"I daresay you know that I was considered unfit to lead a company because the very first time I was put in charge of one I decided to get to the bottom of all those discrepancies in the issuing of rations. You see, my first day as C.O., each man was supposed to receive twenty-five grams of butter. A straightforward calculation: ten men one package, simply. But oddly enough there was one package for every twelve men. At the time my company, including all subordinate units, consisted of a hundred and eighty men. That meant that, at fifteen times twelve men, somewhere along the line a pound and a half had gone astray. I immediately summoned my quartermaster-sergeant, and his excuse was that deliveries had been short. In his presence I phoned the fellow in charge of provisions at battalion headquarters, and he admitted that he had had to short two packages per company because that was all he had received. So my quartermaster-sergeant had already kept back one package; at least I had my hands on *him*—it's always easy to catch the small fry. I still had to clarify how it was possible for the division to have short-shipped five pounds of butter for the five ration-drawing units of our battalion.

"I kept phoning those guys till they almost went out of their minds, I made them spend hours recalculating, and it turned out that each unit had actually had to be shorted three pounds because the butter had turned rancid. Replacements were promised. After a phone bombardment of almost two days I finally had the battalion quartermaster on the hook with a shortage of two pounds. So far so good. Now just figure out how many battalions, sections, ration-drawing units, there are to a division. Oddly enough, for the next three days full rations were issued. Butter and margarine seemed to have lost their tendency to turn rancid. But I persisted. On the fourth day, a shortage again. This time, company and battalion quartermaster-sergeants had clean hands. Wherever a shell explodes close by, people are scared, but farther back. . . . Well, I had a phone. You can imagine how those fellows hated me; I was relentless. If one of the men told me something had gone bad, I contacted his superiors and asked whether this had been reported

and whether the facts had been investigated. But I
got nowhere. It didn't work. The soldiers never received their full rations for more than four consecu-
tive days. The funny thing was that I also became
unpopular in my own company; the topkick and the
sergeant were scared and thought I was crazy. Luckily
I had won a few officers over to my side. I would
phone, or write a report, every day if so much as a
single gram of jam was short. Well, the upshot was
that I personally punched the divisional quartermaster in the nose: I need hardly tell you that fellow was
fat as a bedbug in an overcrowded barracks. The
officers let me down, saying it was futile to fight the
administration, it was a clique, and so on."

He swallowed some coffee, picked up the bread
again, put it down again.

"Well," he went on, "I was powerless, of course.
At the hearing I was accused of being senselessly
fanatical, quixotic. The divisional quartermaster
emerged from the battle a rosy, innocent lamb. I was
duly punished, transferred, and narrowly escaped
demotion. But damn it all, I can think of no more
meaningful battle than against the administration, for
the administration—*any* administration—is the administration of mindlessness, the administration of
the administration—oh, God! I'd like to take over
the administration of life! I'd like to represent the
rights of the living against those dead creatures, even

if during my next attack I have to throw my insignia
in the general's face. I don't want them!" he suddenly shouted, then, embarrassed, began stirring his
coffee although it contained neither milk nor sugar.
With a sigh he raised his head: "Now it's starting all
over again," he said. "You can help me. Do you want
to?"

"Sir," I said, blushing, "my conscience isn't suf-
ficiently clear for me to accuse others of filching."

"No?" he merely asked.

I told him about my finaglings in Paris. He listened with lowered head; my confessions clearly embarrassed him.

"You see," I added, after outlining the essentials,
"wherever I can cheat the state, I have no scruples.
The state has stolen six years of my youth, it has prevented me from learning a trade. I would call that
'getting compensation.'"

"So," he asked quietly, "you wouldn't hesitate to
sell a bicycle, for instance, and pocket the proceeds?"

"Absolutely not," I admitted, "although . . ."

"Although?"

"Although several years of concentration camp
seem an excessive price to pay for a bicycle."

"So it's only the punishment that deters you?"

"Yes."

"That's interesting," he cried eagerly. "Most
interesting! This is the first time I've heard that put

in such classically cynical form. Nevertheless," he
went on with a smile, "if you thought there was the
slightest chance of somebody being personally
harmed, you wouldn't take anything, would you?"

"No," I said.

"We shall see," he said. "I have to go on duty
now." It was eight o'clock. He ate his scrambled eggs
and bread, swallowed a few more mouthfuls of coffee, and left.

Half a minute later I left the house, without having touched my breakfast.

At eight-fifteen I stopped outside the quiet tavern
where, barely a week earlier, I had seen and spoken
to the girl. It was so quiet all around that I had to
stand still and listen. I think that for the first time in
my life I could hear my heart beating—rapidly
pounding away, that invisible hammer in my
chest. . . .

Very quietly I propped the bicycle against the
wall and walked straight through the open gate into
the yard, for after dismounting I had heard the gentle sounds of milking. I saw her at once, and she, too,
having heard my footsteps, had risen and turned
around. There she stood: milk dripping from her fingers as they hung, curved inward, by her sides, her
hair tied back smooth and tight, her red lips open in

surprise, her grubby gray smock slipping off her left shoulder. She recognized me immediately and stood there motionless as I walked toward her.

Without a word I put my arms around her, and for half a second I felt her hair against my cheek and her warm breath on my neck, but when I turned her head toward me to kiss her I realized that her body was cold and stiff in my arms, and her face, which I could now see, registered such resistance and fear that I was shocked.

"Angel," I whispered to her in German, mad with pain, "angel—I love you!"

Her lips grimaced: *"Laisse-moi,"* she implored, *"je ne t'aime pas."*

I released her instantly, but she did not step back: she just stood there, and I could see she was on the verge of tears. Tears over me. My face must have expressed intolerable pain.

She pitied me, and when I realized that, could see it in her face, I knew for the first time how much I loved her. Even her pity seemed like a gift.

"Angel," I stammered again, "angel!"

I turned away, but she called me back with a strange, birdlike sound. She was smiling. "Wouldn't you like something to drink?" she asked.

Without waiting for a reply she walked past me, wiped her hands on her smock and, with a gesture of extraordinary grace, pulled her smock up over her shoulder. Dazed, with drooping shoulders, I followed her into the house.

I looked at my watch: twenty past eight. Five minutes had passed, and the world had almost come to an end; a last, soft red glow hung over the horizon, for what lover will ever cease to hope?

She had uncorked a bottle and filled two glasses. "I'm thirsty," she said in a low voice. "The air's so sultry, although it's early yet."

I find it hard to describe her smile: it was affectionate and sad, leaving me no spark of hope, yet not coquettish. It was ineffably human—I know no other word. She raised her glass, I nodded and drank.

The wine was delicious, cool and dry, and her face showed that she found it refreshing.

"Yes," I finally said with an effort, my muteness weighing on me like a heavy burden. "If I could just see you occasionally . . ."

We put down our glasses, and I followed her as she led the way outside. One more nod from her, and she was gone.

At eight-forty-five I was at battalion headquarters; the other dispatch bearers were already assembled. I sat on the steps outside, surrounded by that know-it-all chatter, and the time passed incredibly fast. Again and again I dug around in my memory, resurrecting the scene in the barn in order to find some tiny hope, but I found nothing, and yet . . .

We waited a long time. We smoked, walked up and down, sat down again, and I joined listlessly in the general scuttlebutt; it was almost eleven when we were summoned to the orderly room. We were each handed a dispatch box, flat, locked wooden boxes for each of which there was one key with the battalion and one with the company, thus ensuring that we couldn't discover the contents of the dispatches. Nevertheless, it was obvious we were going to Russia. Normally that would have struck me as the ultimate horror; that day it left me cold. I felt numb. I saw the world and didn't see it. I was aware that the weather had become even more sultry, that the sky was covered with heavy gray clouds. Somehow my will-power had also ceased to function. Deep down in a layer of buried consciousness I knew that I must stop, dismount, rest, and try to come to my senses, but I believe I would have gone on riding my bike to the end of the world, on and on, obsessed by the stupefying mechanics of pedaling . . . on . . . on. . . . I was dead.

A terrifying clap of thunder roused me. That same instant a warm, heavy rain started coming down in torrents. I looked about me and recognized my surroundings: there was the group of trees, *her* house, and no other shelter in sight. I raced toward the

house, dismounted, left my bike lying on the ground
and, carrying the box, burst into the corridor.

I left the door open and stood there without making a sound.

Our bond with nature is closer than we realize.
I don't know how long I stood there; I was barely
conscious. When I came to again I realized I was
crying.

The beauty of the torrential summer rain, the cos-
mic power invested in all flowing water, created in
my being some sort of parallel; an element of release,
of flow, touched me. I wept. The unspeakable agoniz-
ing spasm was relaxed, and I was alive again.

With trembling nostrils I breathed in that mar-
velous, sweetly moist fragrance that rose like clouds
from the meadows.

I wept. . . .

Suddenly I heard the footsteps of two people approaching along the flagstone path that skirted the
house. The rain had let up a bit. I winced, as if a
long, fine needle had unerringly pierced the very core
of my sensitivity: they were your brother's footsteps.
We know the people we live with better than we imagine: they were his footsteps. I stood stock still, leaning
against the wall in the darkness of the corridor.

With the girl beside him, he entered my field of
vision, and it was no surprise to me to see her with
him. He was pushing his bicycle, half leaning on it,

his face turned toward me; of the girl, I could see only her back, her head, slightly bent, and a narrow segment of her soft cheek, and I knew that she was smiling. His face was pale and serious, and there was a kind of blissful pain in it, but the shattering thing was the naturalness with which those two seemed to belong together: uttering not a word, merely exchanging little smiles, that gentle pair simply belonged together.

I can't say I felt jealous. I was breathing heavily, suffused with the pain of being totally excluded. They scarcely moved, they just looked at each other, and there I stood: transfixed to the damp wall of that dilapidated house, thinking that it might feel good to die.

Finally he bent down, kissed her, and said: "*Au revoir, Madeleine.*" He quickly turned away and, pushing his bicycle, walked toward the gate.

"*Au revoir, au revoir!*" she called after him.

Then she took a few steps back, probably so as to gaze after him for as long as possible from the top step, and in doing so she bumped against the closed half of the door, turned slightly, saw me, and gave a little shriek. . . .

Your brother had not yet reached the gate. He rushed back to the door; the girl was still looking at me in horror and disbelief. Now he was quite close, saw me, and instantly grasped the situation.

"Come along," he said to me huskily. I followed him like a condemned man, the dispatch box under my arm, retrieved my bike outside the gate, mounted it, and rode off at his side.

We didn't look back.

▲9▲

Neither of us ever saw her again.

We rode in silence to company headquarters, where we parted without a word. He went to his quarters; I had to deliver the dispatch box, then go to the kitchen to collect our midday meal, I having, as always, handed in our mess kits in the morning.

I put my bike in the shed and stopped by the kitchen to receive our two portions of potatoes and stew; then I followed him to our quarters.

He stood up as soon as I entered. He had already brought out the plates from the kitchenette and placed them on the table, also the cutlery, but he tended to do that a bit awkwardly so I put our two mess kits on the tray and calmly rearranged forks, knives, and plates, straightened the loaf of bread, and removed the wilted stalks from the flowers in the vase.

All this time he was pacing up and down with folded arms.

"We can eat now," I said calmly, when everything was ready.

"All right," he said, and at that moment we looked at each other again for the first time; reluctantly I had to smile. He shook his head, his expression registering bewilderment, then shrugged his shoulders; I was still waiting for him to sit down.

"We don't want to pass over this in complete silence," he said in a low voice, "but it's up to you whether we discuss it or not."

"No," I said, my voice equally subdued, "I'd rather not discuss it."

"Fair enough," he said. We sat down, and I passed him the little ladle we used for serving ourselves from the mess kits. There was a knock at the door. Putting down his spoon he called out: "Come in!" and the topkick entered. His normally placid face showed agitation.

By next morning we were on the train heading for Russia. The reports and orders I had picked up were already superseded, canceled by telephone instructions. The men to be transferred had to be selected and prepared for departure that same day and wait at the bases for their replacements, which were said to be on their way. The trucks bringing the replacements were then to take the transferred men to an

assembly point near Abbeville, where a division had
already arrived, been loaded onto the train, and left.
But the train had been blown up, casualties had been
heavy, and the division was a hundred and twenty
men short of combat strength. Your brother and
Schnecker were among the officers.

Whereas I had nothing to do but keep an eye on
our two packs, your brother didn't have a minute's
peace. At the last moment the transferees' clothing
and equipment had to be replenished, and men who
had suddenly been taken violently ill had to be persuaded that they were in fact fit; men about to go on
leave had where feasible to be replaced. Above all,
the transferees had to be assembled as soon as possible in Pochelet so they could attend divine service.

The Catholic divisional priest arrived by car
shortly before four and, in view of the general chaos,
was accommodated in our quarters. I had to endure
his company for half an hour, until the arrival of the
first penitents, to whom I offered the use of my room
while they waited. Meanwhile your brother told me
to clear the living room for the celebration of Holy
Mass and the administering of the Sacraments. So I
found myself alone with the priest for a while. He
had the smooth, rosy skin befitting a staff officer in
France, and the mild and obliging manners of a wine
salesman. When I threw out a few remarks about war,
corruption, and officers in general, he gently rotated

one hand in the other, felt constrained to remove his
cigarette from his lips and, with a bland expression,
said: "Yes, there is much wickedness in the world."

We were interrupted when the first penitent
knocked at the door, saluted stiffly, and came in.

I couldn't help muttering to myself: "*Ave, Caesar,
morituri. . . .*"

The priest looked at me with a smile. He finally
abandoned his cigarette and said: "Well, well, a Latin
scholar!"

His gentle look was a signal for me to leave the
room.

Out in the garden all was quiet. Mild autumnal
warmth was interspersed with cool air, the sky was
blue, and the cottages of Pochelet slept behind their
high hedges and fences. Your brother had driven over
to Larnton, to try and talk some sense into a young
soldier apparently overcome by violent cramps.

Preparations were complete, all the other transferees were ready, and divine service was expected to
begin punctually at five. The Protestant clergyman
was due any minute.

I strolled slowly along behind the company buildings as far as the crossroads and for the first time
entered the Pochelet tavern. It was a single-story, flat-
roofed building, a typical outdoor summer restau-
rant, with its wooden walls and garden chairs. The
big room was deserted; through the open door to the

kitchen I could see the landlady and her husband at their evening meal. She was a pretty, blond woman, with a barmaid's cold beauty. Still chewing, she emerged from the kitchen, gave me a friendly smile, and handed me the bottle of white wine I had requested and for which I didn't yet know how to pay.

"Give me another," I said with a laugh. "Then I won't have to bother you again at your supper." She gave a cautionary little smile, hesitated half-teasingly, but then, having made up her mind, reached in under the bar and brought out another bottle.

I sat down at one end of the room, aware of that terrible despair in abandoned places of entertainment that creeps toward one from each corner. There was a smell of dust, of summer dust.

I couldn't possibly miss the departure; the road outside the window would bring the men from Larnton and the northern bases right past my nose.

I had a whole hour in which to forget the girl's face, to say good-bye to France, and to drown the soft, pink, well-preserved corpselike face of the priest.

That yellow wine is the most exquisite of all; it is like honey and fire, like light and silk, and it's my belief that God caused it to grow in order to keep alive the memory of Paradise in this depressing den of vice that calls itself human society. The more I drank the more I became conscious of a serenity such as I had never known, a serenity amounting almost to wisdom. It is wonderful to drink oneself to sleep, to sink into the arms of that kindly brother of Death.

I remember being able to persuade that cool but sweetly smiling woman to let me have two more bottles in exchange for my watch.

I woke up to find myself on a foul-smelling truck, closed my eyes again in horror, and finally became fully awake at the railway station in Abbeville, beside a troop train on the point of departure. Your brother's laughing face was bent over me.

"He looked," I said, "he looked like a wine salesman. . . ."

"Sure, sure," he said quietly. "Come on now, get up."

I got to my feet and was assigned by him to a column of fourteen men in the process of being incorporated into a company on the troop train.

We traveled across France, past the shining vineyards of the Rhineland, through central Germany, Saxony, Silesia, Poland. The railway stations became ever more gray and dismal, the soldiers ever more desperate and cynical. Gradually we started meeting trainloads of wounded, trainloads of prisoners; the ragged population of the occupied territories crowded around our train. The last of our French matches were bartered for eggs, blankets from French houses transformed into butter, parts of equipment exchanged in the darkness of ghostly railway stations for bacon or tobacco, for even during the transport our rations remained miserably inadequate.

The weather had turned cold, it being now almost the middle of October, and we dragged our long greatcoats through the dirt of Ukrainian stations where tractors were being hurriedly loaded for shipment back to Germany, or where we were held up to allow a transport of severely wounded soldiers to pass along the blocked section.

I didn't see your brother that often. Sometimes, during a brief halt, he would come to our car and chat with us, and on rare occasions, during a longer stop, we found an opportunity to take a stroll together. We never spoke of the past. It was an overcrowded, inadequately locked chamber whose bolts must never be touched.

Sitting side by side next to the buffer stop of a siding or on a damp stack of railway ties, we tried to feel our way toward the mystery that was awaiting us, that neither of us knew: the front line. For the farther we were hauled into this dark land, the clearer it became that nothing we encountered here would be comparable to the kind of war we had been experiencing in France. Here anything wearing a gray uniform was filled with a frightening urge to get as far to the rear as possible.

This army had never recovered from the shock of that first disastrous winter. The wounded with whom we spoke were waiting tensely for the train to move on, farther back, without stopping. Every minute in this country seemed wasted; all they wanted was to get farther back from the front, not only quickly but also as far back as possible. It was painful to listen to their illusions on the subject of Germany. Would that country, now also dirty, mangled, wretched, and starving, where barracks had become prisons and hospitals had become barracks—would that country live up to their dreams?

A week later we stopped at a fair-sized station said to be not far from the headquarters of Army Group South. Here, after being fed miserable rations (supplied in France) throughout the journey, we were suddenly provided with an excellent meal: there was some good soup, plenty of meat and potatoes, and at the end a distribution of candies, schnapps, and cigarettes.

There was even champagne, and I was lucky enough, when lots were drawn, to win a whole bottle that we had been meant to share. It was very cold, the stove in our car glowed, and I can well remember opening the train door a crack and, while I looked out, drinking up the bottle as I absentmindedly filled and emptied, filled and emptied, my mug, at the same time breathing in the icy air. I felt stupefied.

Having enjoyed all those delicacies, we suddenly found ourselves being unloaded, and after lining up we started out on a long, wearisome march to the nearest airfield. That was in the afternoon.

Next morning, while it was still dark, we launched our first attack.

What a glorious ring there is to those words: to launch an attack! It sounds like a fanfare, seems to tell of keen young warriors who—in obedience to the stratagems of war—can barely suppress the song on their lips as they attack, attack with exultant hearts.

We, by contrast, had deplaned in early-morning darkness and had to suffer grievously for our premature insobriety. Crammed tightly together in trucks, half suffocated by weapons and packs, we had been driven toward the front line and spent a further two hours in strange houses in a strange village. Each sound coming from the nearby front triggered new fears, it being impossible to relate such sounds to anything one had previously experienced. Thus I was scared over and over again by the sudden high-pitched bark of an antitank cannon that seemed to be positioned right behind our building. Each time I believed that Russian tanks were at our door, and each time I experienced mortal fear.

The light in that little room where we all huddled together had gone out, and when things finally quieted down I simply leaned back in the darkness, searching among shoulders, legs, heads, and weapons for a bit of space, and closed my eyes. A vile stench filled the room. Apparently a barrel of pickled cucumbers had begun to ferment and had burst; the floor was awash with a disgusting, reeking liquid, and our groping hands kept touching the soft, nauseating objects strewn around. I smoked incessantly, if only to keep down my nausea; no one said a word. We had imagined it all quite different, not quite so bad and not so terribly sudden.

It was still dark when we were ordered outside, where to my joy I recognized your brother's voice. The little yard was packed with soldiers, as I could see when the red flash from a cannon briefly illuminated it. A company: that word represents so many living souls, so many destinies, yet how much did a company amount to on this front!

Your brother explained, briefly and seriously, that he would be in command of us, that we had been ordered to seal off a breach. Truly a task for novices! It was appallingly difficult to organize the company in the dark, to hand over the groups and platoons to their respective leaders. I was called out by him and could tell by the grip of his trembling fingers when he grabbed me by the sleeve that he, too, was scared.

"You stay with me," he said huskily.

Well before dawn we left the village, guided by a sergeant from the staff of the regiment to which we

had been assigned. Oh, what a long way we still had
to go to reach the actual front! A relief, at least, to
have earth under one's feet. In front and behind,
seemingly all around us in fact, were gun flares and
detonations. It would have been impossible to determine the battle line from these indications. The sergeant knew nothing for certain, either. Who did! He
told us in a whisper, as we marched along, that a
whole battalion had been taken by surprise here, some
of them killed, some taken prisoner; a few survivors
had managed to escape. It was still uncertain whether
the Russians had occupied the position, or whether,
surprised by their own success, they had merely with-
drawn with booty and prisoners to their own positions.

Strangely enough, those constant detonations
didn't bother us much. What was terrible was the dark
silence lying ahead of us, and we had to march into
that darkness until we met resistance or reached the
old positions. It was our job to determine the actual
battle line, if possible to reoccupy the old positions
and hold them.

There were four of us in the lead. Your brother
and the sergeant in front, while I followed with a
corporal. Sometimes when I think back to those days
I believe that war is an element. When a man falls
into water he gets wet, and when a man moves around
at the front, where infantrymen and sappers dig
themselves into the ground, he is in the war. That

atmosphere is an acid test: there are only good fellows and bad; all intermediate categories either fail or rise to the occasion.

My instinct told me: the N.C.O. walking beside me was a bastard. He was a coward, saturated with fear and abandoning himself to it without resistance. The way he flung himself to the ground when your brother or the sergeant softly passed on the command was enough to tell me that he would be capable of anything. There was something uncontrolled, something brutish, about the way he immediately hurled himself down and hugged the earth. The sergeant was very calm; he radiated a quality that can only be called courage, a spiritual aura stronger than fear.

Meeting no resistance, not even from rifle fire, we reached the line where on both sides was a lively exchange of fire while ahead of us there still seemed to be that dark, silent cotton batting that was going to absorb us.

The sergeant's hearing was fantastically accurate. From among all those sounds, small and large, he pinpointed the one: that of a Very flare pistol being discharged. He dropped instantly to the ground, the signal for us to hiss the command to those behind us so we would no longer be visible in the brilliance of the silver flash.

At each flare I would try to recognize something, but there was only the dark, black earth, with many,

many indistinct mounds that could just as well have been plowed furrows as crouching men.

My God, how often have I wondered at the immensity of the power that—despite cowardice and fear—induces millions of men to stagger passively on toward death, as we were doing that night.

We reached the old positions, meeting no resistance and suffering no losses. For the first time we trod in the dark on corpses; for the first time we prepared ourselves for a potential enemy lying in wait for us eighty or a hundred yards away. Everything had to be done incredibly fast. Before daybreak the platoons had to be at their battle stations, the rest of the men in their positions, and contact had to be established with the units on our left and right that had not fallen back.

Perhaps this so-called front is imagined as a straight line, drawn with a ruler on a map by a general-staff officer. Actually it is a very tortuous affair, receding and projecting, a highly irregular snake that adapts to the terrain or is forced by enemy pressure onto unfavorable ground.

How much we had to do in a single hour if daylight was to find our defenses prepared! On the right, no contact could be established. A corporal and two men sent out to look for the nearest German sentry on the right never came back: we never heard or saw anything of them again. Another patrol, accompanied by your brother, moved a bit farther back and discovered that we had advanced much too far on the right. The whole line had to shift and adjust, and all that in total silence, in the dark, in a terrain pockmarked by shell holes. Corpses lay all around—Germans and Russians; weapons, parts of equipment. . . .

The company battle station was located almost in the center of the sector, slightly to the rear. There were two bunkers, each with space for three men. Telephone communication had been cut off. Try to imagine the state of mind of a telephone operator who has been sitting for three years in a hotel room in France, connecting the banal chitchat of the various staffs: now he is in Russia, in a situation fraught with danger, and has been ordered to repair and check the telephone line, half an hour before dawn.

The sergeant was a quiet, slight man, pale and unshaven. The usual decorations dangled casually from his chest. His job done, he stayed on with our group long enough to smoke a cigarette. We hardly spoke, but when he stood up to say good-bye he said with a smile—it sounded almost like an apology: "I'm due to go on leave tonight." He slung his machine pistol on his back, shrugged his shoulders, and shook hands all around; then he drew aside the blanket that shielded the bunker toward the rear.

The next moment he lay dead at our feet.

The shell struck the escarpment of the trench, the dark sky seemed to collapse, the light had gone out, the corporal screamed like a madman; and when, covered with clods of earth and fighting down my fear, I raised myself forcibly, I touched a bleeding body, my hand sank into a foul, wet mass, and I screamed too. Meanwhile your brother had drawn the blanket across again, and switched on his flash-light, revealing a ghastly sight. The legs of the dead sergeant stuck out from under the blanket, into the bunker, the corporal's right leg had been severed below the knee, our cigarettes were still alight: your brother held his between his lips.

"Bandage him," he told me, his face pale. He stepped outside.

The artillery barrage continued. We became familiar with the sound of Russian mortars, the horrible whine of the heavy artillery shells that seemed to be driving death before them. While the earth trembled all around us, I bandaged the whimpering corporal. With some vague notion of making a tourniquet, I rashly tore off my suspenders—the next day I would have taken his since by then he no longer needed them, whereas for me there were occasions later when the lack of them almost cost me my life. I made a tourniquet around the stump and wrapped gauze and rags, as many as I could find, over the bleeding wound. When I tried to leave the bunker, the wounded man clung to me, but I had made up my mind to die under the open sky and I pushed him away.

Outside, the darkness was lit up by brief red flames; it looked as if fire were leaping from the earth, fire instantly to be covered by darkness again.

That short barrage seemed to go on forever. I thought the entire Eastern Front must be in turmoil, a giant offensive under way. Actually it lasted—your brother had checked it on his wristwatch—seven minutes and was comparatively harmless. The company's casualties were four dead and seven wounded.

We were all totally exhausted: the rigors of the train journey, the march, the flight, and again the journey by truck—and now this concentrated encounter with the front. But we were to learn that there was no longer any such thing as sleep, although there were hours when one simply sank into oblivion, slept as if dead, was dragged to one's feet, stood sentry or was sent off to one of the other platoons as a dispatch runner.

In those first nights—during the day it was hardly possible to move outside our sector—I invariably lost my sense of direction. There I would lie, stretched out on the earth, darkness all around, waiting for a flare to go up that would allow me to recognize some landmark that would tell me whether I had to crawl forward, backward, or sideways. Sometimes, when

I eventually crawled off, I was aware in that singing, cold silence of something eerie, something indescribable, like an invisible, inaudible yet palpable breath: the proximity of the enemy. I would know then that I was quite close to the Russian positions, and often a hoarse whisper or call, a terrible alien laugh, confirmed that I was not mistaken.

Oh, that fear of being taken prisoner by the Russians! It was this fear alone that prevented the war in Russia from ending as early as 1942. Imagine, if you will, what would have happened if our soldiers had been made to fight there for years under the same inhuman conditions, the same incompetent leadership, against the Americans or the British.

We remained in that sector for one week.

▲10▲

THE ATTACK expected for the morning of the following day did not come until evening. During this attack, something occurred that I would never have believed possible: we repulsed it.

From the moment I saw the first shapeless, muffled-up figures really and truly a hundred yards away from us approaching our sector—from that moment on I stood totally prepared to flee, my whistle

at my lips, braced against the rear wall of the trench,
one hand poised for the leap. Your brother stood there
quite calmly, giving the orders that we had to pass
on. Every few seconds we had to duck when a wave
of Russian fire seemed to burst right in our faces,
and every time that appalling fear when one could
raise one's head again: Are they here?

From time to time I would look back to make sure
of a retreat under cover, for one of the old soldiers
had told me, between two gulps from a bottle of
schnapps: "What matters most in this whole war,
kiddo, is a retreat under cover."

The Russians came surging forward, forced over
and over again by the scythelike action of our
machine-gun fire to fling themselves to the ground:
the screams of the wounded were already filling the
thick gray air. From the rear we were supported
by heavy artillery, while the neighboring companies
also aimed their fire in front of our sector. Still, it
seemed hopeless to try to stem that relentless tide.
Just then your brother suddenly gave the order: "Pre-
pare to attack!" Hardly had he uttered the command
when a heavy salvo of Russian naval guns forced us
to take cover. I ducked, and it flashed through my
mind: This is it, you can't go back, by now the Russians are here. But suddenly your brother's voice
shouted: "Forward, charge!"

He was the first to go over the top: with a fren-

zied gesture and another shout, he swept the entire
company after him, and charge forward we did. At
first the Russians hesitated, but that moment was
enough; first a few of them started running, then
whole groups turned tail—we could hear the shrill
yelling and cursing of their officers while the rest put
up their hands. We brought back twenty prisoners,
the first living Russians we had seen face to face:
their eyes held only one thing—fear.

The evening of the eighth day I was sitting, for
the first time in a long while, alone with your brother
in the bunker. While we waited tensely for the ration-
runners, we drank schnapps and smoked cigarettes.
The stretcher-bearer had gone back with the ration-
runners to pick up medicines, bandages, and anti-
tetanus ampules, for if anyone was wounded in
daytime we had to leave him lying where he was until
nightfall. Your brother sat by the phone, and I
squatted at his feet on the flattened pile of straw on
which we slept.

"The whole secret of attack," he suddenly said,
after we had been silent for a long time, "is to imagine how scared the enemy is. Imagine yourself crouching in your hole and you suddenly see some characters
charging at you and yelling their heads off! You go
crazy with fear, you saw that on Tuesday, we lost all
self-control. You have to force the enemy to become
passive. Then he's done for."

"You've found the secret of how to win the war," I said drily. "Sell it for a fortune, and you've got it made."

He gave a quick laugh, then his expression grew serious again, and he lit another cigarette. "But the terrible thing is that one doesn't know which side one wants to win. . . ."

At this moment the stretcher-bearer rushed in, shouting: "We're being relieved, sir, we're being relieved!"

What was happening was that the front, whose defense was demanding increasingly pointless sacrifices, was being shortened; the lines were allowed to shrink, and for several days a few units could be saved that were then sent back to the front to reinforce the shortened line. Whatever the reason, it was wonderful to go back to the rear for at least a brief respite. The ration-runner hadn't bothered to bring any more rations; we were to have our meal in peace and quiet at the rear. At midnight, when darkness had become solid, we moved off, a sad procession: one week earlier we had moved into position with nearly eighty men, and we were returning with forty-eight.

In the dark it was impossible to make out whether it was the same place. When we actually did reach the village I was filled with a fantastic feeling of life.

Your brother was kept busy for a while, making

sure his men were properly accommodated, supervising the distribution of rations. He gave orders that the following day the men would be off duty, attended to a pile of tiresome paperwork in the orderly room, and instructed me to heat up enough water for a thorough wash.

We were billeted in a farm cottage whose rough windows had been nailed up with cardboard and then draped with blankets. I lit four bunker lights, one in each corner, and stoked up the stove with plenty of wood. It was almost November. I had lost all desire for sleep, although an hour earlier I could have collapsed from exhaustion. Slowly savoring every mouthful, I emptied my mess kit, washed down the rich bean soup with generous swigs of schnapps, and stuffed the larger of my two pipes so full of tobacco that the pale yellow shreds hung over the edge. Drawing deeply on my pipe, I would drink another schnapps and watch the roaring flames as they devoured the wood in the stove. From time to time I would dip my hand in the bucket to test the heat of the water. With every pull on my pipe I sucked in something precious, indescribable, something that felt good even as I remembered the dead and the wounded: life.

When the water seemed hot enough I carefully pulled out my underwear from the bag I had col-

lected from the company baggage, chose a decent
civilian shirt—light blue with a proper civilized col-
lar—and sniffed it: it still smelled of Cadette's soap.

Slowly, with an intoxicated sensuousness, I
washed myself. Imagine if you can: you live in the
ground and receive every day as much or as little
liquid as you need to barely satisfy your most ele-
mentary thirst; not a single opportunity to wash even
your fingertips, yet still having to spend hours crawl-
ing over the wet ground. You become matted with
dirt. Fortunately, since we were all newcomers, we
had been spared the otherwise inevitable lice, those
demoralizing vermin that contributed significantly
toward our losing the war. Later I was to become
familiar with them.

I kept on washing long enough for the fresh lot
of water to have heated up again; then I shaved and
put on clean underwear and socks. I was filled with
exaltation: never had that rotgut tasted so delicious,
never had tobacco tasted so good. Just before two,
your brother came back. He greeted me wearily, sat
down on the bench by the stove, removed his cap and,
with a sudden gesture, flung it onto the floor in the
middle of the room.

While he ate, I set the bucket of water on a low
wooden stool, put soap and towel beside it, and laid
out the underwear I had taken out of his pack.

Then I lay down on a bed in the corner and

watched him. When he began to shave I said: "You still owe me the solution to a riddle you asked me at the station in Abbeville. About the wine salesman . . ."

"Yes," he said with a laugh, "that was two weeks ago, it feels as if it had been in another life."

"It was in another life," I said.

"Maybe you're right—I'll give you the solution before the day is out."

The door opened, and in came Schnecker. We were surprised less at the sight of him than of a new decoration on his chest.

I had jumped to my feet and accorded him the mandatory obeisance. With a wave of the hand he said: "Lie down again."

Your brother greeted him silently and, just as silently, offered him a stool.

Schnecker seated himself astride a chair, lit a cigarette, and proceeded to watch your brother shaving.

I had ample time to observe him as he sat turned sideways toward me. He sat extraordinarily still, almost motionless, but when I looked at him more closely I realized that he was completely drunk. He was at that stage when a drunk man is filled with a leaden stability, when an almost idiotic law of gravity keeps him upright. When he started to speak, it became obvious that I had assumed correctly.

"My friend," he began; his voice, very pinched,

came from high up in his throat. "I see you're up to some nice little tricks, my friend, hm?"

"What do you mean?" countered 'your brother, who had finished shaving. He dried his face and put on his shirt.

"I see you're up to some nice little tricks. I haven't heard a thing about there being no duty to-morrow, and you simply go ahead and order it." He laughed.

Your brother laughed, too. "If you haven't heard a thing about it, so much the better."

"But now I have heard about it," said the captain, his tone sharpening as he jerked himself to his feet. "And I'm telling you that it's important for the men to go over their weapons and gear tomorrow—the day after that we're being redeployed, assigned to the Seventeenth, a bit farther south, understand?" By now he was almost shouting.

"I understand perfectly, but first I'm going to see that the men get some sleep. Besides . . ." He hesitated, slowly tied his neckband, ran his hand once more over his hair, looked at Schnecker, and was silent.

"Besides what?" asked the captain.

"Besides," your brother calmly continued, "I would have preferred it if I could have seen you now and then up at the front with me this past week."

"What's that?" A wary look came over the captain's face, and he shot a glance in my direction, but I had closed my eyes and pretended to be asleep. The two men now lowered their voices.

"I would have preferred it if I could have seen you now and then in my sector during this past week. It would have given the men quite a boost, and me too, for that matter. It's dreadful to feel all the time that one is alone. After all, orders are only paper."

"Paper?" asked Schnecker. His expression was now almost maniacal, his voice had slipped, too, and he was now quite hoarse.

"Yes, paper!" shouted your brother, so loud that I was really startled. "Paper! Paper! A substance inferior even to that gilt tin on your manly chest!"

"Oho!" cried the captain; now he was laughing again. Suddenly he stood stiffly to attention. "I have to inform you, First Lieutenant Schelling," he said raspingly, "that you have been awarded the Iron Cross First and Second Class, also the Infantry Assault Medal in Silver. You fought damn well. In fifteen minutes the gentlemen of the battalion will be holding a small celebration in your honor and"—he gave a little bow to himself—"in mine, too."

He put on his cap and marched out stiff as a ramrod. It was almost as if he hadn't been there at all. Your brother whistled softly as he cleaned his nails, the cigarette between his lips. I rose and put out two of the lights that had begun to flicker and threatened to burst into flames.

"I don't feel much like sleeping now—how about us looking in on the party?"

"Us?" I asked in surprise.

"Of course you're coming along—you're getting a decoration, too, maybe a couple."

"What, me?" I exclaimed.

"Of course," he laughed, "besides, there'll be women there. I'd like to have one more chance to see a woman."

"Girls?" I cried.

"Maybe girls, too!" He laughed again. "I've no idea what kind will be there. Anyway, they'll be women, and I'd like the chance to have a glass or two of wine with one of them."

"Jesus!" I cried. "Women!"

He stood up and drew on his greatcoat. I put on my cap and slipped into a padded camouflage jacket.

We stepped out together into the cold night; it was quiet, something resembling peace lay spread under the dark vault of the sky. Headquarters were in a large building, something between a palace and a manor house—I imagine it had been the administrative offices of a kolkhoz.

The sentry let us pass without hindrance, although we didn't know the password. We found ourselves walking along dark corridors and managed to rout out a telephone operator who directed us to the third floor. Raucous singing filled the corridor, which smelled of Russia. A door opened, light and noise streamed out onto the corridor, were immediately swallowed up again, and we soon came upon a figure that was staggering toward a window, apparently to throw up.

"Hullo, Piester!" cried your brother. The man turned, recognized your brother, and waved. We went closer. He leaned on a windowsill and groaned pitifully. It was the adjutant, an agreeable young lieutenant not much given to talking.

As we stood beside him he said: "I can't take any more, Schelling. He keeps forcing me to drink, I can't take any more, but he threatens to shoot anyone who won't drink. I can't take any more." He leaned over the sill, I followed him with my eyes; below lay a dark, silent garden that appeared to be planted with vines.

"Where's your room?" asked your brother.

"Why do you ask?"

"Come along."

Your brother took Piester by the arm and steered him ahead down the long corridor. Each time Piester hesitated, your brother gave him another push. Piester opened a door.

"Let's have some light," your brother said to me. I fished out my box of matches, and by the light of the burning match we entered the room. Then I closed the door behind me and ran to the window to fasten the blackout curtain.

The room looked bare. On the floor lay a pack, beside the narrow wooden bed stood an officer's trunk, and on it a half-written letter and a candle stuck to the lid. A piece of broken mirror hung on the wall.

We forced Piester onto the bed; his face was yellow.

"Something terrible is going to happen," mumbled Piester, his eyes closing the moment he lay down. "He's run out of schnapps, and the paymaster won't fork out any more. Something terrible—they're expecting you . . ."

We went back onto the corridor. All this time I had been listening, almost apprehensively, for a woman's voice, but even now I could hear nothing but that stupid male yowling.

The moment we opened the door, silence fell in the room. It was a scene of utter debauchery: Schnecker was sitting on the table, his legs spread-eagled, his tunic unbuttoned and revealing curly black hair

on his broad chest. Beside him stood an artillery officer holding a bottle of Cognac upside down over
Schnecker's gaping mouth. After a brief pause they
both resumed their bestial yowling.

Over in the corner stood the battalion's medical
officer, an elderly bourgeois type; beside him a young
Russian woman with soft blond hair and a rosy,
peasantlike face: she looked like a girl. I assumed
her to be the doctor's mistress, a doctor herself, of
whom I had heard a good deal when collecting our
rations. She was said to be very skillful at bandaging
and very kind to the wounded. Now she was watching
the scene at the table with a completely dispassionate
curiosity, while her lover, looking very nervous, was
holding her tightly by the arm.

"Good evening, gentlemen," said your brother.

Schnecker let out a hoarse roar and tried to jump
off the table, but he slipped and would have struck it
headfirst if we hadn't caught him in time. The artillery
officer smashed the empty bottle onto the floor and
looked at us idiotically.

"Good evening," your brother repeated, smiling
in the direction of the Russian woman, who bowed
slightly and smiled back at us.

We helped Schnecker down from his wedged position on the table. "Not a drop of booze left!" he
shouted. "Goddammit, not a drop left, my good
friend Karlemann has just squeezed the last drops

out of the bottle for me!" He gratefully patted the
artillery officer, who was still laughing idiotically.

"Well!" said your brother. "You're a fine host,
I must say: when I arrive there's nothing left!"

Schnecker stared at him. Those bloodshot eyes
were hot and ugly.

I could look only at the Russian woman; the mere
sight of her soft, rosy skin gave me a pang of happiness, and I trembled as she approached. She kept her
eyes firmly on Schnecker as she took her doddering
old medical officer by the hand and walked without a
sound to the door.

Meanwhile Schnecker had been having an incoherent, raucous dialogue with the artillery officer, but
when the Russian woman was almost at the door—I
had stepped aside and was close enough to be aware
of how crisp and clean she smelled—Schnecker swung
around in a flash and, his mouth agape with laughter,
shouted: "Stop, my girl—not yet! You have to have
another drink with me!" The medical officer had freed
his hand and stepped back.

"But you've nothing more to drink!" said the
woman, her voice as clear as ringing metal.

"There's more on the way!" He careened around
the table, guffawed, dashed to the door, flung it open,
and screamed: "Alarm! Alarm! Alarm!"

At first we didn't understand and stood rooted to

the spot. Even the artillery officer seemed to have sobered up a bit. Schnecker came back and called out to us: "Now he'll have to get out of bed, that stinker— then we'll have some booze!"

Your brother sighed and took a deep breath, flung himself at Schnecker, and thrust him out into the dark corridor. I followed them, the woman screamed, the medical officer shouted: "My God . . . my God . . . ," while the artillery officer tried in vain to get around the table, stammering: "Karlemann . . . Karlemann . . ."

Schnecker was now wrestling outside with your brother: he was a muscular fellow, and drunkenness must have doubled his strength. I ran to them, grabbed him from behind, and dragged him over to the window, meanwhile pummeling away at him in my towering rage. Somewhere in the dark the last of his decorations fell with a tinny sound onto the tiled floor. Schnecker groaned, spat, bit, and, whenever he managed to free his mouth, which your brother was clamping shut, screamed like a madman: "Alarm! Alarm!"

When an orderly came up from downstairs and asked what was going on, your brother called out to him: "Nothing, he's drunk." By this time we were pretty close to the window, but now the artillery officer had also slipped through the door and was attacking your brother from behind; furthermore, a staff sergeant came running along the corridor shouting: "What's going on? What is it?"

"Alarm!" yelled Schnecker. "Alarm!"

"Nothing," shouted your brother. "He's drunk!"

He now had Schnecker by the throat, while I had tripped the artillery officer and was preventing him from getting up.

Schnecker had been forced over to the window. He was groaning and seemed to be bleeding somewhere. "Don't you realize, you bastard," your brother said to him, "that the other hundred and twenty men in your battalion can use a few hours' sleep?"

Schnecker, who by this time had freed himself, yelled even louder: "Alarm! I am ordering alarm!" And when your brother, suddenly seized by a sort of frenzy, punched him right in the face, Schnecker, in a lightning move, drew his pistol, held it to your brother's temple, and pressed the trigger. Your brother was dead on the spot: he fell to the floor across the whimpering artillery officer. Schnecker had turned pale, his hand was still holding the pistol. There was an eerie silence: I was about to fling myself on him, but at that moment the first Russian tank started firing outside the building. We stared at each other. Hideous bursts of firing shattered the sky. Schnecker had already run off down the corridor. I dashed after him but on the way ran into Piester's room and

shouted in his ear: "The Russians are here—move!"
Then I ran down the stairs to the ground-floor corridor and jumped out the window into the garden.

I managed to escape and from a distance saw the
great building in flames. I kept running until I was
scooped up by another regiment and sent back to the
front. Not one man from our unit escaped. The Russians had overrun the village from three sides and in
great numerical superiority. And although I never
saw Schnecker again, or was ever told, I knew he had
managed to get away. He can't die. I assumed that in
some way or other he would inform your mother of
your brother's death. He has done nothing. He just
goes on living. All this I learned during the last few
days.

I pass the truth on to you. It belongs to you. . . .

A NOTE ABOUT THE AUTHOR

Heinrich Böll is the first German to win the Nobel Prize for literature since Thomas Mann in 1929. Born in Cologne, Germany, in 1917, Böll was reared in a liberal Catholic, pacifist family. Drafted into the Wehrmacht, he served on the Russian and French fronts and was wounded four times before he found himself in an American prisoner-of-war camp. After the war, he enrolled at the University of Cologne, but dropped out to write about his shattering experiences as a soldier. His first novel, *The Train Was on Time*, was published in 1949, and he went on to become one of the most prolific and important of the postwar German writers. His best-known novels include *Billiards at Half-Past Nine, The Clown, Group Portrait with Lady,* and *The Safety Net*. He is also famous as a writer of short stories. The year 1984 saw the publication of *What's to Become of the Boy? or Something to Do with Books,* his memoir of growing up in Germany in the years 1933 to 1937. Böll is past president of International P.E.N. and is a leading defender of the intellectual freedom of writers throughout the world.

A Note on the Type

This book was set on the Linotype in Bodoni Book, named after Giambattista Bodoni (1740–1813), son of a printer of Piedmont. After gaining experience and fame as superintendent of the Press of the Propaganda in Rome, in 1768 Bodoni became the head of the ducal printing house at Parma, which he soon made the foremost of its kind in Europe. His *Manuale Tipografico*, completed by his widow in 1818, contains 279 pages of type specimens, including alphabets of about thirty languages. His editions of Greek, Latin, Italian, and French classics are celebrated for their typography. In type designing he was an innovator, making his new faces rounder, wider, and lighter, with greater openness and delicacy, and with sharper contrast between the thick and thin lines.

Composed by
Maryland Linotype Composition Company,
Baltimore, Maryland.
Printed and bound by
The Maple-Vail Book Manufacturing Group,
York, Pennsylvania.
Designed by Marysarah Quinn,
based on a design by David Connolly.